Praise for *November*:

"*November* is profoundly interesting for the light that it throws on the close relationship between Flaubert's life and his writings. It is a work of capital importance."
—*Times Literary Supplement*

"*November* is both beautiful and moving. It describes those Arabian Nights flights of youthful imagination that desire strange and distant lands and visions of splendour. It is a work of art."
—*Saturday Review*

November

GUSTAVE
FLAUBERT

November

Carroll & Graf Publishers, Inc.
New York

Reprinted by arrangement with McIntosh & Otis, Inc

First Carroll & Graf edition 1987

Carroll & Graf Publishers, Inc.
260 Fifth Avenue
New York, NY 10001

ISBN: 0-88184-334-2

Manufactured in the United States of America

November

"When November's haze engulfs the blue sky
How the forest whirls, how the leaves fall.
Oh, my muse! then into my soul you creep
Like a shivering child approaching the hearth."

VICTOR HUGO

INTRODUCTION

It is probable that most readers of this translation of Flaubert's early novel, *Novembre*, have come to it by way of the first of his great novels, *Madame Bovary*. In the United States and England, translations of *Madame Bovary* are many times more widely read than those of any of Flaubert's other major works—*Salammbô*, *L'Education Sentimentale*, the three short tales, and *Bouvard et Pécuchet*. There must be thousands, perhaps hundreds of thousands, of readers of *Madame Bovary* in English who have never read, perhaps never heard of, another work by Flaubert. Those reading *November* for the first time have probably read *Madame Bovary* and have probably opened *November* out of curiosity.

They are almost sure to be taken aback.

November, although concerned in at least as large a part as *Madame Bovary* with "illicit love", and although abounding in psychological observation and in valid maxims, and although written in beautiful, Chateaubriand-like French prose, has little of the "readability" that makes the later work so spell-binding. The particular power and readability of *Madame Bovary* were its great and novel attractions when it appeared in 1857, and they were achieved by a thousand technical devices contrived by a mature genius—economical profusion of detail, controlled style, constant shifting of scene, focus, and angle of view, dramatization of confrontations, and a host of others, from the most obvious to the amazingly subtle. Most of them have been used, or attempted, or deliberately eschewed, by writers of novels ever since. It has often been said that with *Madame Bovary* Flaubert "invented" the modern novel. Certainly his stamp is still on it, to such an extent that avant-garde novelists, like children of a genius father, are constantly struggling against its hold on their minds and their craft, and constantly expressing their resentment of its dominance in abusive language. Meanwhile it continues its insufferably triumphant career. It persists in being, for novelists, what Henry James calls a "lion in the path"—difficult if not impossible to get around, and dangerous.

November is not dangerous.

Flaubert himself recognized it as being not dangerous enough to publish. He was nineteen and twenty when he wrote it. At that time, it was much the best thing he had done, and he was, and always remained, both proud and ashamed of it. Unlike his still earlier productions (he had begun to compose as soon as he could write), which he showed to almost no one, he read or lent the manuscript of *November* to numerous friends. A "sentimental and amorous mishmash", he called it in a letter to a former teacher. "The action is nil. I wouldn't know how

8

to give you an analysis of it, since the whole thing is psychological analyses and dissections. Perhaps it is very beautiful, but I'm afraid it may be very false and rather pretentious and stilted." When he was thirty-two he wrote to his mistress, Louise Colet, "I re-read *November* Wednesday out of curiosity. . . . It is not good, there are monstrosities of bad taste, and it does not hang together satisfactorily. I see no way of re-writing it; it would have to be done over entirely. There is a good sentence here and there, a good comparison, but no *tissu de style*. *November* . . . will stay in my portfolio indefinitely. Ah! How farsighted I was not to publish it in my youth! How I would blush for it now!" In his forties he thought sufficiently well of it to read it aloud to the Goncourt brothers. But it was printed only posthumously.

And yet *November*, though it lacks force and readability, and threatens not a hair on the head of the most susceptible novelist today, is an important and interesting little book, the like of which any artist could scarcely help but be glad to have written.

The Flaubert who finished *November* on October 20, 1842, shortly before his twenty-first birthday, was an unwilling student of law in Paris, with years of stormy adolescence just behind him. (In one sense the turbulence was to culminate only later, in a year or two, when a series of nervous seizures, similar to epilepsy in their manifestations, cut short his legal studies, ended any possibility of an "active" career, and "condemned" him

9

to the sedentary existence he greatly desired.) A sensitive, and especially a literary, adolescent in the Romantic period in France was apparently doubly prone to agitation: in addition to all the normal physiological and nervous strains, the spirit of the age left him no peace. Flaubert's earlier works bear such titles as *Death of the Duc de Guise*, *Two Coffins for an Outlaw*, *The Fiancée and the Tomb*; and just before *November* he had written *Agonies*, *The Dance of Death*, *Drunk and Dead*, and *Memoirs of a Madman*. Those were fashionable titles at the time. It was an age much marked by the macabre, like our own—except that to us ours seems much more authentically ill-starred.

It was in the classical setting of the French *collège*— the Collège Royal de Rouen, in his native city—that Flaubert had passed the turmoil of his adolescence. His particular turmoil had two unusual external manifestations: his writing, many of the aspects of which were a good deal more precocious than his titles suggest, and participation in a student revolt against the *collège* itself —a defiance of authority demanding approximately n times as much "sincerity" as any such demonstration today. As a graduation present his family offered him— he was eighteen—a trip to the south of France, Malta and Corsica under the aegis of a certain Dr. Jules Cloquet. Dr. Cloquet had been a fellow-student of Flaubert's father in medical school, and as departure became imminent Dr. Flaubert wrote to his son: "Profit from your

trip, and remember your friend Montaigne, who thinks
that one should travel chiefly in order to bring back the
humours and customs of other lands, and to '*frotter et
limer notre cervelle contre celle d'autruy.*' Watch, observe,
take notes: don't travel like a grocer or a salesman."

Lucky son, of such a father!

When the travellers reached Marseilles, Dr. Cloquet
revealed to his young companion his acquaintance with
certain ladies. These were no less than the owners of the
hotel at which the tourists stopped, Madame Eulalie
Foucaud, née De Lenglade, and her mother, joint pro-
prietresses of the Hotel Richelieu, rue de la Darse.
Apparently Dr. Cloquet chose the Hotel Richelieu because he already knew the ladies. Perhaps, knowing
them, knowing the daughter especially, it occurred to
him that he might do his travelling companion a favour.
In any case, on a certain late-summer Saturday night, the
eighteen-year-old Gustave Flaubert, who had hitherto,
according to his own later testimony to the Goncourts,
"merely lost his virginity with his mother's maid,"
learned about *volupté* from the thirty-five-year-old
Eulalie Foucaud. She was not a prostitute, like Marie
the whore with the heart of gold in *November*, but a
respectable married woman, with an absent husband, a
little daughter, and interests in South America; however, the *volupté* she enabled the young traveller to
experience that hot night in Marseilles must be that
evoked in the second part of *November*, where the

modern reader, who has long been asking, "Isn't anything going to happen?" is finally rewarded.

We know from Flaubert's recently published notebooks* how very closely, during adolescence, he resembled the nameless "hero" of *November*, who as the story opens portrays himself at fifteen. Flaubert was filled with the same dreams of women, the same longing for affection and *volupté*, the same self-pity—that self-pity that so characterized sensitive youth in the Romantic age. They had read *Werther*, and they felt an intense need for consolation in the face of a barren bourgeois world. Then, in part two of the book, the nameless hero is eighteen, Flaubert's age at the time of the adventure in Marseilles, and Flaubert has the young man describe the satisfying of his adolescent sensuality at that age in terms that echo adolescent writings done by himself, Flaubert, earlier, before the 1840 journey.

But: beware! Gustave Flaubert, the author of *November*, written in 1841–42, has in the meanwhile become a novelist, a novelist in bud but a novelist; he is no longer writing his notebooks, but a piece of fiction, and he is no longer the adolescent he had been only a year or two before. The long-awaited experience of sensual pleasure set off in Gustave Flaubert—who hap-

* Gustave Flaubert, *Souvenirs, notes et pensées intimes*, Avant-Propos de Lucie Chevalley Sabatier. Buchet/Chastel, Paris, 1965. (To be published by W. H. Allen as *Intimate Notebook, 1840-1841*.)

pened to be a genius—a process of release never vouch-safed the sad, untalented hero of *November*. Since the *volupté* of Marseilles, Flaubert had begun to frequent prostitutes. By the time he writes *November* he has more "first-hand material" to draw on than merely whatever it was that Eulalie Foucaud had to tell him. It has been suggested that the life-story of Marie, that "set piece" conventionally inserted into *November*, sounds as though it might be based on reminiscences recounted by one or more acquaintances of a single night—no doubt embellished both by Flaubert's memories of his own earlier Romantic readings and by his increasingly mature observations. And the sentiments of Marie's eighteen-year-old nameless partner in sensuality (who remains much as he was when he was fifteen) must be taken as a kind of *historical* writing—writing about what was now for him an earlier, previous stage of sensibility—by the rapidly maturing twenty-year-old Flaubert.

Then, at the end, the subjective-objective complex becomes still subtler. Using another conventional device, this time the venerable dodge of the discovered manuscript, Flaubert, now writing no longer in the guise of his nameless hero, but in that of the discoverer of the manuscript, his hero's friend, turns openly on his hero—turns, that is, on himself as he was when he was fifteen, perhaps up to eighteen, when he had his adventure in Marseilles: he turns on his own Romantic past. "From his earliest youth he had fed upon extremely bad authors, as will have been seen from his style"; "He was a man prone to fallacy and rigmarole, and he greatly misused epithets." So much for his past writing: down the drain! And at the same time his picture of the later years of his weakling-hero is a sympathetic one. It becomes a self-portrait again—"Resigned to boredom everywhere and in everything, he declared that he wished to study law and went to live in Paris"—and the poor fellow turns out to be too good for this world. He dies—Flaubert kills him off with a death whose improbability he underlines—he makes him just fade away. It must have been difficult and painful to decide just *what* to do with him: how dispose of your dead past when it's inseparable from your living present? "*November*," Flaubert wrote Louise Colet, "was the end of my youth."

Unlike his nameless hero, Flaubert did not fade away. His nervous attacks soon freed him from law school; and the rest of his life, apart from a few travels, he spent in his native Normandy, writing his novels. At first the objectivity about his past so prominent in *November* was not sufficient to keep him from writing a little more "fallacy and rigmarole", and from misusing a few more epithets. It took him ten years to come to the undertaking of *Madame Bovary*.

It is in *November*, however, that *Madame Bovary* is most clearly foreshadowed. Many are the scenes, the descriptions, the portrayals of human traits, the epithets, that are re-used in the later, greater novel. A copy of

Madame Bovary in which reminders of *November* were printed in a type different from the rest of the text would be a strange, patchwork sight.

"*Madame Bovary, c'est moi,*" Flaubert is supposed to have said, when asked about the "original" of his heroine. It has often been shown how the "moi" in question was the adolescent Flaubert, the schoolboy in love with Romanticism, filled with yearnings, who longed to taste of *volupté*, and, a little later, when he had tasted it, discovered what Jean Bruneau has called "the fundamental problem of 'Bovarism', that life does not correspond to men's desires, that happiness does not exist". We know what Flaubert did, after his experiences with *volupté*: he turned his back on "living" and wrote his books in country solitude. And we all know what happened to Emma Bovary. It becomes obvious to the reader of *November* that the clearest prototype of the two of them —more precisely, the clearest early mirror-image of Flaubert, and the clearest prototype of Emma—is the nameless, Romantic, unhappy hero of this youthful novel, who just fades away after wearing so many of Flaubert's old clothes—and some of his new ones.

A word about the translation, which seems to me an excellent one. Mr. Frank Jellinek, now well known for his study of the Paris Commune and a translator of much experience, has written me about how it came to be done: "It was the first large-scale translation I ever did from

French—my languages in those days (about 1932) being Greek, Latin, German, Spanish, Icelandic, Anglo-Saxon, Gothic and French, strictly in that order. So far as I can recall the origins, I did it as a more or less privately-printed job for a nice man called Ernst Reichl in exchange for a rather good Rolleiflex camera and about fifty dollars (fifty dollars on the barrelhead just about kept one off the breadline for a month in those days). About the same time I bought some ablebodied seaman's papers off an un-ablebodied chap in a speakeasy, and the translation was done in pencil somewhere off Peru (we were about the last steamer to go through the Straits of Magellan), sent off at odd South American ports—no airmail in those days, unless Saint-Exupéry was functioning then—with the idea that I'd revise in New York when I got back. I never did get back that year or the next. . . . There are undoubtedly some mistranslations—to this day I recall trying to find a French dictionary in Valdivia to see what Flaubert meant exactly by 'terroir'. . . ."

In view of Mr. Jellinek's distance, at that time, from dictionaries—which he quite properly qualifies as "useful adjuncts, though no substitute for wide reading in the literature of the particular language"—he has kindly allowed me to make a few substitutions in his text, which was indeed originally published by Ernst Reichl in 1932. But I wonder whether that casual manner of working—by a young man who was, of course, better versed in French than he now pretends—may not have been in part responsible for the graceful freedom of this translation, its fine rhythms, its air of being English romantic prose rather than a translation at all.

FRANCIS STEEGMULLER

"Pour . . . niaiser et fantastiquer." *
MONTAIGNE

* "To be foolish and fantastic . . ."

I love autumn: the sadness of that time of year agrees well with memories. When the trees have shed their leaves, when the sky at twilight still holds the russet glow that tints the faded grass, it is pleasant to contemplate the extinction of all that was aflame within us.

I was returning from a walk over the deserted meadows and along the frozen canals, the willows' mirror. The wind whistled in the stripped branches; now it sank, now all at once it rose again, then the little leaves still clinging to the bushes fluttered, and the grass shivered as it bent to the ground. The world seemed to grow more pallid, more frozen. The sun's disc on the horizon was lost in the white blankness of the sky, tingeing the air around it with a trace of expiring life. I was cold, and almost frightened.

I sought shelter behind a mound of turf. The wind had fallen. I do not know why; but as I sat on the ground there, thinking of nothing and watching the smoke rise from the thatched cottages in the distance, my entire life appeared, ghost-like, before me, and the bitter scent of the days that are no more came back to me with the smell of the dried grass and the dead trees. As if the winter

19

were driving them before it in a wailing tempest, my poor years swept past me again, some terrible power whirled them through my memory with a fury greater than that which was harrying the dead leaves down the still pathways; some strange ironic power lightly edged them, turned them over and over before my eyes, then drove them all off and away until they were lost against a sombre sky.

It is sad, this time of year. You might imagine that life is setting with the sun. A shiver trembles over your heart as over your flesh. Every noise dies down, horizons grow pale. Everything is preparing for sleep, or for death.

After a while, I saw the cows coming home, lowing as they turned toward the setting sun. The little boy who herded them before him with a bramble shivered under his sacking. The cows slipped in the mud as they went down the slope, crushing a few apples left in the grass. The sun cast a last farewell from behind the dissolving hills; lights sprang up in the houses down the valley; and the moon, the moon of the dew, the moon of tears, began to show her pallid face between the clouds.

Long I savoured my lost life; joyfully I said to myself that my youth was over; for it is a joy to feel the cold creep over your heart, to be able to say, as you test it with your hand as you might some still-smoking hearth, "it is no longer afire." Slowly I reviewed all my past life, the ideas and the passions, the days of ecstasy and the days of grief, the thrill of hope and the agonies of despair.

I saw it all again, as a man visiting the catacombs slowly contemplates, ranged on either side of him, the dead on the dead. By count of years, it is true, it is not long since I was born: but I have innumerable memories whose weight crushes me as old men are crushed by the weight of all the days they have lived. Sometimes I feel that I have lasted out centuries, that my being holds the relics of a thousand past existences. Why? Have I loved? Have I hated? What have I sought? Still I do not know; I have lived withdrawn from all movement, all action, bestirring myself neither for glory nor for pleasure, neither for knowledge nor for wealth.

No man has ever known anything of what follows: those who saw me every day knew no more than the others; they were, in relation to me, as the bed on which I sleep, which knows nothing of my dreams. And indeed, is not the heart of a man a vast solitude into which nothing ever penetrates? The passions that enter it are like travellers in the Sahara: they stifle and perish and their cries are unheard by the world outside.

At school I was melancholy, restless, seething with desires; I felt ardent aspirations towards a wild and turbulent existence: I dreamed of the passions and wished to know them all, all. Beyond my twentieth year I saw a whole world of lights, of perfumes; before me in the distance was Life with its splendours and triumphal shouts: it was like a fairy-tale, where in gallery after gallery diamonds glitter beneath the fire of golden chandeliers, a magic name rolls enchanted doors back on their hinges, and as you advance, your eye plunges into magnificent perspectives so dazzling that you can only smile and close your eyes.

I coveted some vague splendour which I could not have formulated in any phrase or defined in any precise form, yet I had a positive and incessant desire for it. I have always loved bright things. As a child, I used to push my way among the crowd at the fairground to gaze at the scarlet braid of the attendants and the favours on the bridles of their horses; I would stand for hours in front of the jugglers' tent, staring at their baggy trousers and their embroidered collars. Ah! and most of all I loved the tightrope dancer, the long pendants in her ears swinging to and fro about her head, the great jewelled necklace thudding on her breast. Uneasily, avidly, I watched her as she leaped as high as the lamps strung between the trees, and her dress, edged with golden spangles, swished and swung and bellied out upon the air.

Those were the first women I loved. I tormented my imagination dreaming of those strangely-formed thighs so firmly encased in pink tights, those supple arms wreathed in bangles—the bangles that they rattled against their backs when they bent backward so far that the plumes of their turbans touched the ground.

Woman, whom I was already trying to divine (and there is no age at which we do not dream of women: as children, we squeeze the breasts of the big girls who kiss us and hold us in their arms, with a childish sensuality; at ten, we dream of love; at fifteen, we find it; at sixty, we have it yet; and if dead men dream of anything in their graves, it is to creep underground into the next grave, lift a dead woman's shroud and share her sleep)— woman, then, had for me the attraction of mystery, and that troubled my poor child's mind. From the sensation I experienced when one of them chanced to let her eyes rest on me, I felt already that there was something fatal in that stirring gaze which melts the human will, and I was at once charmed and terrified by it.

What was I dreaming all those long evenings of study as, elbow on desk, I would gaze and gaze at the lamp-wick lengthening in the flame and the oil falling drop by drop into the cup, while my school-fellows' pens scratched on the paper and from time to time there came the rustle of turning pages or the noise of a book being shut? I used to hurry to finish my tasks so that I might give myself up at leisure to these cherished musings. Indeed, I would promise it to myself beforehand with all the attraction of a real pleasure. As a poet who wishes to create provokes his inspiration, so I would begin by compelling myself to think of it; I would go as far as I could into my thought, revolve it in all its aspects, penetrate to its farthest depths; then I would return and begin again. Soon it became an unbridled career of the imagination, a prodigious soaring out beyond reality; I made up adventures for myself, composed stories, built palaces and dwelt in them as emperor, plundered the mines of all their diamonds and strewed them in great handfuls over the road I was to traverse.

And when evening came and we were all in our white beds with their white curtains and only the master on duty was walking up and down the dormitory, then I shut myself yet more closely away within myself, deliciously hiding in my breast this bird with beating wings and a warmth that I could feel. It was long, always, before I fell asleep; I would listen to the hours striking, and the longer they were, the happier I was. It seemed to me that they were singing as they carried me on into some other world, that they were saluting each moment of my life with: "On to others! On to others! It is to come! Farewell! Farewell!" And when the last vibration had died away and my ear no longer hummed with its sound, I would say to myself: "Till tomorrow; the same hour will strike, but tomorrow there will be one day less, one day further towards that world beyond, towards that shining goal, towards my future, towards the sun—its beams flood me now, but then I shall hold it in my hands"; and I said to myself that it was very long in coming; and I fell asleep almost in tears.

Certain words set me in a turmoil: especially "woman" and "mistress". I sought the explanation of the former in books, and in drawings and pictures from which I longed to tear away the draperies to discover what lay beneath. On the day when I finally divined all, I was stunned at first with a delight like a supreme harmony, but soon I became calm, and I lived thenceforward with greater enjoyment; I felt a stirring of pride when I told myself that I was a man, a being organized to have, one day, a woman of my own. I knew the password to life; and that was almost to have entered it, to have tasted something of it already: my desire went no farther and I remained satisfied with knowing what I knew. As for a mistress, she was to me a satanic being: the magic of the word alone threw me into long ecstasies. It was for their mistresses that kings conquered and ruined provinces; for them were woven the carpets of the Indies, for them gold was wrought, marble chiselled, the world overturned; a mistress has slaves with feather fans to drive off the midges when she sleeps on satin sofas; elephants laden with presents await her awakening; palanquins carry her luxuriously to fountain-brims; she lolls on thrones in a radiant and fragrant atmosphere, far from the crowd whose execration and idol she is.

The mystery of the wife without marriage, who is yet the more wife for that, excited and tempted me with the double allurement of love and riches. I loved nothing so much as the theatre; I loved it all, to the buzz of the intervals and the corridors through which I sped with pounding heart to find a place. When the performance had already begun, I would race up the staircase, would hear the sound of the instruments, the voices, the applause, and when I took my seat the whole air was

fragrant with a warm odour of well-dressed woman,
something that suggested the bunch of violets, the white
gloves, the embroidered handkerchief. The galleries be-
decked with people, like so many diadems of flowers and
diamonds, seemed suspended in the air to hear the singing. The actress was alone, to the fore of the stage, and
her bosom rose and fell as the notes poured forth head-
long; the rhythm urged her voice on, carried it off in a
whirlwind of melody; her roulades made her swelling
throat undulate like the neck of a swan, beneath the
weight of aërial kisses; she stretched out her arms; she
was crying, weeping, scintillating, calling to something
with inconceivable love, and when she took up the motif
again, the sound of her voice seemed to tear out my heart
and confound it with hers in a spasm of love.

They flung her applause, they flung her flowers, and
in my ecstasy I felt myself sharing with her the adoration
of the crowd, the love of all those men and the desire of
each one of them. It was by her that I wanted to be loved,
loved with a devouring and terrifying love, that love of a
princess or an actress that fills us with pride and makes
us the equals of the rich and the mighty! How beautiful
is the woman whom all applaud and all envy, the woman
who gives the crowd the fever of desire for their nightly
dreams, the woman who never appears but by candle-
light, radiant, singing, moving in the ideal world of the
poet as if it were the life made for her! On her lover she
doubtless bestows another love, one yet more beautiful

than that which she pours out in floods on all the gaping hearts that quench their thirst with it, songs far sweeter, notes far deeper, far more amorous, more tremulous! Had I been able to approach the lips from which issued those pure sounds, to touch the shining hair radiant beneath the pearls! But the footlights seemed to me the barrier of illusion; beyond them lay the universe of love and poetry; there the passions were more beautiful, more melodious, forests and palaces dissolved like smoke, sylphs descended from the skies, all was song, all was love.

Such things as those I mused on alone in the evening when the wind whistled along the passages, or in the hours of recreation when the others were playing at prisoners' base or ball, as I sauntered along the wall, treading in the fallen linden leaves for the pleasure of hearing the sound of my feet lifting and shuffling them.

Soon I was seized by the desire to love; I longed for love with a boundless avidity, I dreamed of its torments, I expected every moment an agony that would fill me with joy. Several times I believed I had it. In my thoughts I would take the first-met woman who seemed to me beautiful and would tell myself, "She is the one I am in love with," but the memory of her that I longed to retain would grow paler, and vanish instead of increasing, and indeed, I felt that I was forcing myself to love, that I was trying to trick my heart but in no way succeeding in doing so, and this failure was a lasting sadness: I almost regretted loves I had not had, and then I dreamed of others with which I longed to be able to fill my soul.

Especially on the day after a ball or a play, or on my return from a two-or-three-day holiday, I would dream of a passion. I would picture my choice as I had seen her, in a white dress, whirled away in a waltz on the arm of her smiling cavalier, or leaning on the velvet ledge of a box, calmly displaying a regal profile. The bustle of the quadrille, the glitter of the lights resounded and dazzled me a while, then all dissolved into the monotony of a melancholy reverie. Thus I had a thousand little loves that lasted a week or a month though I longed to protract them for centuries; I do not know of what these vague desires consisted nor on what end they converged; it was, I think, the need of some new emotion, and an aspiration, as it were, towards something higher, the summit of which I was unable to discern.

The puberty of the heart precedes that of the body; I had more need of loving than of enjoying, more desire for love than for pleasure. Today I cannot even imagine the love of first adolescence, when the senses are nothing and the infinite alone holds sway; coming between childhood and youth, it is the transition between them and passes so quickly that it is forgotten.

I had read the word Love so much in the poets and had repeated it to myself so often to charm myself with its sweetness, that to every star that shone in a blue sky on a gentle night, to every murmur of the stream against its banks, to every ray of sun on the dewdrops I would say "I am in love! Oh, I am in love!"; and I was happy, I was proud, I was ready for the finest acts of devotion, and above all, when a woman brushed me in passing or looked into my face, I wished I might love her a thousand times more, be even more at her mercy than I was; I wished my heart would throb so violently as to burst my breast asunder.

There is an age, as you will remember, reader, when you smile vaguely as if there were kisses in the air; your heart swells in the fragrant breeze, your blood beats warm in your veins, it sparkles like wine bubbling in a crystal goblet. You wake up happier, richer than the night before, more lively, more excited; sweet saps rise and sink in you, impregnate you divinely with their intoxicating warmth, the trees toss their heads in the wind in soft curves, the leaves shiver one against another as if they were talking together, the clouds glide by, laying open the sky in which the moon, smiling, mirrors herself in the river from on high. As you walk in the evening and breathe the scent of cut hay and listen to the cuckoo in the wood and watch the racing stars, is not your heart purer, more bathed in air, in light, in blue than the peaceful horizon where the earth meets the sky in a tranquil kiss? Oh, the fragrance of women's hair! The softness of the skin of their hands, the penetration of their gaze!

But already it was no longer the first dazzlements of childhood, the agitating recollections of the dreams of the night past; now I was entering a real life in which I had my place, an immense harmony in which my heart and the hymn that it sang vibrated magnificently: I savoured with joy the charm of this expansion, and my awakening senses doubled my pride. Like the first created man, I awoke at last from my long sleep and saw beside me a being like myself but endowed with other qualities which set between us a dizzy attraction, and at the same time I felt for this new form a new emotion which filled my mind with pride, and the sun shone more purely, the flowers were more fragrant than ever, the shade was softer, more caressing.

At the same time, each day I felt the development of my intelligence: it lived a life in common with my heart. I do not know whether my ideas were emotions, for they had all the heat of passions; the intimate joy I felt in the depths of my being flowed over the world and made it fragrant with the excess of my happiness, for I was on the point of attaining the knowledge of supreme delights, and, like a man at his mistress's door, I prolonged my yearning on purpose that I might savour an assured hope and say to myself: "In a moment I shall hold her in my arms, she will be mine, mine utterly, it is no dream!"

Strange contradiction! I fled the society of women, and yet in their presence experienced a delicious pleasure; I boasted that I loved them not at all, whereas I lived in all of them and longed to penetrate the essence of each that I might become one with her beauty. Already their lips invited me to kisses that were not maternal, in imagination I wrapped myself in their hair, I pressed myself between their breasts to suffer a divine suffocation; I longed to be the necklace that kissed their throat, the clasp that bit their shoulder, the dress that covered the rest of their body. Beyond the dress I conceived nothing; beneath it was an infinity of love, and I would lose myself in the imagination of it.

I studied in books the passions I longed to have. For me, human life revolved on two or three ideas, on two or three words, around which everything else turned like satellites around their planets. Thus I had peopled my infinite with a quantity of golden suns: in my head love-stories were set beside noble revolutions, grand passions beside great crimes; I dreamed at once of the starry nights of tropical lands and the sack of burning cities, the lianas of virgin forests and the pomp of lost monarchies; of tombs and of cradles; the murmur of the stream among the reeds, the cooing of the turtles in the dovecotes, myrtle woods and the scent of aloes, the clash of sword on breastplate, prancing horses, shining gold, the glitter of life, the agonies of despair, all these I contemplated with the same wide-mouthed stare, as if they were an ant-heap stirring at my feet. But over this life, so active on the surface, so resonant of varied cries, there mounted an immense bitterness that was its synthesis and its irony.

On winter evenings I would stop before lighted houses where they were dancing and watch the shadows passing behind the red curtains; I would listen to sounds eloquent of luxury, glasses rattling on trays, silver tinkling on plates; and I would tell myself that it depended only on myself to take my part in this festivity to which all flocked, in this banquet at which all ate; but a savage pride drove me away, for I found that my solitude ennobled me and that my heart was larger if I secluded it from all that made up the joy of other men. So I pursued my way through the deserted streets beneath the arclights that swung mournfully on their creaking brackets.

I dreamed out the grief of the poets, I wept with them their most beautiful tears, I felt them in the utmost depths of my heart, I was rent, torn by them, and I sometimes thought that the enthusiasm I felt for them made me their equal, raised me to their height. Pages that left others cold filled me with ecstasy, with a sibylline fury; wantonly I submitted my heart again to their ravishment, I recited them beside the sea, or said them over to myself as I walked with bent head through the grass, in the most amorous and most tender tones.

He is to be pitied who has not longed for the tragic wrath, who cannot recite love stanzas from memory by the light of the moon! It is glorious to live in such eternal beauty, to parade with kings, to experience passion at its most intense, to love the loves that genius has made immortal.

Thenceforward I lived in an ideal and limitless world, where, flitting free and at leisure, like a bee I garnered from every object some nourishment, some life. I tried to discover in the noises of forests and streams words unheard by the rest of mankind, I strained my ears to catch the revelation and the harmony. I composed with cloud and sun stupendous pictures which no tongue could have rendered, and, equally, in human activities, all at once perceived relations and antitheses whose luminous precision dazzled me. Sometimes art and poetry seemed to open their boundless horizons and to illumine one another with their own splendour. I built palaces of red bronze, I mounted eternally towards a radiant sky on a stairway of clouds softer than swansdown.

The eagle is a proud bird who perches on lofty peaks; below him he sees the clouds roll into the valleys, carrying the swallows with them; he sees the rain fall on the pines, the freshet roll down the marble boulders, the herdsman pipe to his goats, the chamois leap the precipice. In vain the rain streams, the storm shatters the trees, the torrent rolls sobbing down, the cascade leaps in smoke, the thunder bursts and breaks the mountain-peaks: calmly he flies above it all, beating his wings; the clamour of the mountain gladdens him, he utters cries of joy, he struggles with the racing clouds and mounts higher and higher into the immensity of his sky.

I too was gladdened by the clamour of the tempests and the vague hum of men which rose up to me; I lived in a lofty aerie where my heart swelled in the pure air, where I uttered cries of triumph to break the spell of my dull solitude.

I soon felt an invincible disgust for the things of this world. One morning I felt old, full of the experience of a thousand things I had not yet known; I was indifferent to the most tempting, disdainful of the most lovely; all that was the envy of others was pitiful to me; I saw nothing that was worth the trouble of desiring. Perhaps it was that my vanity placed me above the common vanity, perhaps my indifference was only the excess of a boundless cupidity. I was like one of those new edifices on which moss begins to grow even before they are finished building. The tumultuous joys of my companions bored me, and I shrugged at their sentimental absurdities: some kept a white glove or a faded camellia a whole year that they might cover it with sighs and kisses, others corresponded with shopgirls or made assignations with cooks; the former I thought idiotic, the latter grotesque. Then too, good and bad society bored me equally; I was a cynic with the godly and a mystic with the libertine, so that I was not much loved by either.

At this period, when I was still virgin, I took pleasure

in watching the prostitutes. I used to pass along the streets where they lived, to frequent the places where they paraded; sometimes I would talk to them to tempt myself; I would pursue their steps, touch them, move in the aura they emanated; and since I was impudent, I thought I was calm and found my heart empty; but that emptiness was an abyss.

I loved to lose myself in the turmoil of the streets; often I indulged in senseless distractions, such as to stare fixedly at each passer-by in order to discover in his face some salient passion or vice. The heads passed swiftly before me; some smiled, whistling as they went their way, hair blowing in the wind, others were pale, others ruddy, others livid; they slipped rapidly past me, vanished one after the other like signboards when one is driving by. Or else I watched only the feet moving in every direction and tried to attach each foot to a body, each body to an idea, each motion to an object; and I wondered whither all those feet were going, why all those people were afoot. I used to watch the carriages vanish beneath the sounding porticoes and hear the heavy steps unfolded with a clatter. The crowds swirled at the theatre doors, and I watched the lights glisten on the fog while above stretched the inky and starless sky. A barrel-organ would be playing at the corner of the street, ragged children were dancing, a fruitseller plied his barrow lighted by a red flare. The cafés were clamorous, mirrors glittered in the flame of the gas-jets, knives clattered on marble tables. In the doorways the shivering poor stood on tiptoe to watch the rich eat. I would mingle with them, and with a stare like theirs I would contemplate those who were enjoying life; I was jealous of their vulgar merriment, for there are days when one is so sad that one would make oneself yet sadder, when one wantonly buries oneself in despair as being the easiest way, when one's heart is swollen with tears and one urges oneself to weep. I have often wished that I were poverty-stricken, that I wore rags, that I were tormented with hunger, that I might feel the blood flow from some wound, that I might entertain a hate and seek a revenge.

What then is this restless sorrow of which one is as proud as of genius yet conceals like a secret love? You reveal it to no one, you hug it to yourself, you strain it to your breast with tearful kisses. But yet, what is your complaint? Who is it that makes you so melancholy at an age when all smile upon you? Have you not devoted friends? A family whose pride you are, patent-leather boots, a padded great-coat, etc.? Poetic rhapsodies, recollections of trashy books, rhetorical hyperboles: may not all these grand nameless sorrows, and happiness too, be nothing more than a metaphor, the invention of some hour of idleness? I long suspected it: today I suspect no longer.

I have loved nothing, and I longed so strongly to love! I shall die without having tasted any of the good things of life. At this very moment, even human life offers me yet a thousand aspects that I have scarcely conceived.

Never have I heard, as I rode my panting horse by the banks of a lively stream, the sound of the horn in the depths of the woods, never have I felt a beloved hand tremble in mine, press it in silence amid a soft night fragrant with the exhalations of the rose. Oh, I am emptier, hollower, more melancholy than a broached barrel when it has been drunk dry and spiders spin their webs in the dark within.

It was not the sorrow of René nor the celestial immensities of his disquietude, nobler and more argentine than the moon's rays; I was neither chaste like Werther nor debauched like Don Juan: all in all, I was neither pure enough nor bold enough.

I was, then, what you all are: a certain man who lives, sleeps, eats, drinks, weeps, laughs, a man shut up in himself, finding in himself wherever he may go the same ruins of hopes dashed as soon as raised, the same dust of ground-down things, the same a-thousand-times-trodden paths, the same unexplored, terrifying and satiating depths. Are you not as tired as I am of waking each morning, of seeing the same sun? tired of living the same life, of suffering the same sorrows? weary of desire and weary of disgust? weary of expectation and weary of possession?

What is the good of writing this? Why continue the same funereal recital in the same melancholy tones? When I began it, I knew it was good, but as I proceed, the tears fall on my heart and stifle my voice.

37

The pale winter sun! It is as sad as a memory of happiness. Shadows fall all around us: let us watch our hearth blaze; the coals are covered with great intersecting lines which seem to pulse like the veins of some other life. Let us await the oncoming of night.

Let us recall our fine days, the days when we were gay, when we were all together, when the sun shone, when hidden birds sang after the rain; the days when we walked in the garden, when the sand of the paths was damp, when the calyces of the roses had fallen into the borders and the air was fragrant. Why did we not enjoy our happiness enough when it was slipping through our hands? On such days we should have had mind only to taste it, to savour each minute that it might glide more slowly. I recall with delight even certain days that passed like any other. One day, for instance: it was winter and very cold; we had come back from a walk, and since there were not many of us, we were allowed to sit around the stove; we were warmed and at ease and we toasted our bread on our rulers while the stove-pipe rumbled; we chattered of a thousand things: of the plays we had seen, of the women we loved, of our leaving school, of what we would do when we were grown up, etc. Another time I spent the whole afternoon lying on my back in a field where little daisies sprang from the grass; they were yellow and red, and melted into the green of the meadow so that it was a carpet of innumerable shadings. The pure sky was covered with white cloudlets that rippled like waves. With my hand spread over my face I gazed at the sun: it turned the edges of my fingers to gold and my flesh to rose, and I shut my eyes on purpose to see, under my eyelids, great green splashes fringed with gold. And one evening, I have forgotten when, I fell asleep at the foot of a rick; when I awoke, it was night and the stars were shining and twinkling and the hay-stacks cast their shadow behind them, and the moon showed a lovely silvery face.

How far away it all is! Was I alive in those days? Was it really I? Is it I now? Every minute of my life seems all at once separated from every other by an abyss, between yesterday and today I see an eternity which terrifies me; every day I think that I was not so wretched the day before, and, although I cannot say what more I possessed, I feel that I grow poorer and that the coming hour takes something from me, and I am astonished that I still have room in my heart for suffering; but the heart of man is limitless in its capacity for sadness: a happiness or two can fill it, but all the miseries of humanity can gather there and dwell there as its guests.

Had you asked me what I lacked, I should not have been able to reply. My desires had no object, my sadness no immediate cause; or rather, there were so many objects and so many causes that I could not have distinguished one. Every passion found an entrance into me, but could find no exit; they huddled together there and set each other alight as if with concentric mirrors. Modest, I was yet full of pride; living in solitude, I yet dreamed of fame; retired from the world, I yet burned to appear, to shine, in it; chaste, I yet abandoned myself in my dreams, by day and by night, to the most unbridled licentiousness, to the most savage sensualities. The life that I crowded within me gathered over my heart and oppressed it to stifling.

Sometimes, at the end of my endurance, devoured by limitless passions, buried beneath the blazing lava that rolled down from my heart, loving with a fury of love things without a name, longing to recapture dreams of magnificence, allured by all the pleasures of imagination, inhaling the essence of every poem, of every harmony— and yet crushed beneath the weight of my heart and my pride, I would sink, annihilated, into an abyss of agonies: blood whipped my face, my arteries roared deafeningly, my breast seemed on the point of bursting asunder, I could no longer see, no longer feel,—I was drunk, I was mad, I had delusions of grandeur, I imagined that I bore within me some supreme incarnation, the revelation of which was to have set the world agape, and those pangs were the very life of the god that I was carrying in my entrails. To this magnificent god I immolated all the hours of my youth. I had made myself into a temple to receive some divinity; the temple has remained empty, nettles have grown between the stones, the pillars are crumbling and the very owls are making their nests in it.

Since I did not use existence, existence used me; my dreams wearied me more than great labours. A whole creation, motionless, unrevealed to itself, lived mute below my life; I was a sleeping chaos of a thousand fertile elements which knew not how to manifest themselves nor what to be, still seeking their form and awaiting their mould.

The variety of my being was like some immense forest in the Indies, where life surges in each atom and shows itself, monstrous or lovely, beneath each sun-ray. The blue of the sky is redolent of perfume and poison. Tigers leap, elephants march proudly like living pagodas. Mysterious and deformed, the gods are hidden in hollow caves amid huge heaps of gold. And through its midst flows the vast river, with its gaping crocodiles, their scales rattling against the lotus on the banks, and its islands of flowers borne along by the current with tree-trunks and corpses turned green by the plague.

I loved Life, a life expansive, radiant, irradiate. I loved it in the furious gallop of coursers, in the glitter of the stars, in the rushing of the waves towards the shore. I loved it in the surge of lovely naked bosoms, in the flutter of amorous glances, in the vibrations of the chords of the violin, in the swaying of oak-trees, in the setting sun when it turns the windows to gold and calls up thoughts of the balconies of Babylon on which queens rested their arms as they looked towards Asia.

Yet in the midst of it all I made no motion. Amid the

41

many activities which I saw, and even instigated, I remained inactive, as inert as a statue buzzed round by a swarm of flies humming in its ears and crawling over its marble.

Ah, how I would have loved had I loved, had I been able to concentrate on a single point all the divergent forces which recoiled on myself! Sometimes I wished to find a woman at all costs; I wanted to love her, she would be the sum of all life for me; from her I expected everything, she should be the sun of poetry and make every flower blossom, all beauty glow. I promised myself a divine love, I bestowed on her beforehand a halo that would dazzle me, and I vowed my soul to the first woman I chanced to meet in the crowd, and gazed at her in such a way that she should have understood me, should have been able to read in that one look all that I was, and have loved me. I placed my destiny on this hazard, but she passed by like the rest, like the ones before and the ones after; and so I fell back again, more shattered than a torn sail soaked through by the storm.

After such spasms, life opened up again the eternal monotony of the hours that glide and the days that return; impatiently I waited for the evening, reckoned how many evenings stretched before me to the month's end— wished for the next season, for there I saw a sweeter life smiling. Sometimes I longed to shake off this leaden mantle that weighed so heavy on my shoulders, to dull myself with knowledge and ideas; I would work, I would read. I opened a book, two books, ten books; then flung them from me in disgust without having read two lines, and relapsed into the sleep of everlasting boredom.

What should one do in this world? What dream? What build? Tell me, you who enjoy life, who press on towards some object, who torment yourselves for some end.

I found nothing that was worthy of me and equally I found myself fit for nothing. To work, to sacrifice everything to an idea, to a wretched and trivial ambition, to possess a place, a name—what good is it? Fame was nothing to me, the most resounding fame could not have satisfied me because it could never chime with the desire of my heart.

I was born with the longing for death. Nothing seemed more stupid than life, nothing more shameful than to cling to it. Brought up, like all my contemporaries, without religion, I had neither the dry satisfaction of the atheist nor the nonchalant irony of the sceptic. If I occasionally entered a church, doubtless merely to indulge a whim, it was to listen to the organ, to admire the statuettes in their niches; but dogma I did not aspire to, too well I felt myself the son of Voltaire.

I saw other men live, but theirs was a life apart from mine: some believed, others denied, others doubted, others did not trouble about the whole business but went about their affairs, that is, they sold their merchandise, wrote their books, shouted from their pulpits: that was what is called humanity—a shifting surface of malice, cowardice, stupidity and ugliness. And I moved amid the crowd like a torn fragment of seaweed on the ocean, lost amid innumerable waves rolling clamorous to engulf me.

I wished that I were an emperor for his absolute power, for his numerous slaves, for the wild enthusiasm of his devoted armies. I wished that I were a woman for her beauty, I wished that like her I might strip myself naked, let my hair fall to my heels, mirror and admire myself in the stream. I lost myself when I would in limitless reveries, I imagined myself sitting at the noble feasts of antiquity, I imagined myself King of the Indies; I rode to the hunt on a white elephant, I watched Ionic dances, listened to the Grecian wave on the steps of a temple, heard the night breezes in the oleanders of my gardens, fled with Cleopatra on my antique galley. Ah, those follies! Unhappy the gleaner who quits her task to lift her head to the Berlins passing on the highroad! Returning to her work, she will dream of silks and the love of princes, she will harvest nothing more, and return home with her garner unfilled.

It would have been better to have done what all do, to have taken life neither too seriously nor too flippantly, to have chosen some profession and practised it, to have seized one's portion of the common cake and eaten it and said that it was good, rather than to have pursued the melancholy path which I trod in solitude. Then I should not be writing this, or it would be a different story. As I proceed, it grows confused even for me, like a perspective viewed from too far; for everything passes, even the memory of our most burning tears, our most sounding laughter. The eye dries quickly enough, the mouth recovers its composure; I recall nothing more than a long boredom which lasted for several winters of yawning, of desiring to have done with living.

This it was, perhaps, that made me believe myself a poet, for none of the poet's miseries did I lack, alas!, as you see. Yes, once it seemed to me that I had genius, my brain teemed with magnificent thoughts, the style flowed beneath my pen as the blood in my veins; at the first hint of the beautiful a pure melody surged up within me like those aërial voices, formed by the winds, which issue from the mountains. The human passions would have vibrated marvellously, had I touched them. My head was filled with complete dramas, full of scenes of fury and unrevealed anguishes; humanity, from the infant in its cradle to the dead man on his bier, found its very echo in me. Sometimes stupendous ideas flashed suddenly across my mind like those vast flashes of summer lightning that light up a whole town, all the details of the buildings and the squares and streets. I was shaken, dazzled by them, but when I found in others the thoughts and even the very forms I had conceived, I fell straight into a profound discouragement: I had thought I was their equal and I was no more than their imitator! I passed from the intoxication of genius to the desolating sense of mediocrity

45

with all the rage of a dethroned king and all the tortures of shame. On certain days I could have sworn that I was born to the Muse, on others I found myself almost an imbecile; and by continually passing from such heights to such depths, I ended, like all men who during their lives are often rich and often poor, in permanent poverty.

In those days I thought as I awoke each morning that some great event was to be accomplished that day; my heart was swollen with hope, as if I were expecting a cargo of happiness from some far country. But as the day advanced, I lost all courage, at twilight I saw well enough that nothing would happen, and at last night came and I went to bed.

Harmonies of sorrow became established between physical nature and myself. How my heart contracted when the wind whistled in the keyhole, when the gas-jets threw their flare on the snow, when I listened to the dogs baying the moon!

I could see nothing to which I might attach myself, neither the world nor solitude, neither knowledge nor impiety nor religion; I wandered amid them all like a soul which hell rejects and heaven repulses. Then I would fold my arms, regarding myself as a dead man, for I was no more than a mummy embalmed in my own sorrow. The fatality which had bowed me from my earliest years seemed to me to spread over the whole world. I watched it manifest itself in men's activities as universally as the sun on the earth's surface. It became an atrocious deity whom I adored as the Indian adores the moving colossus which passes over his body. I began to enjoy my grief, I made no further effort to escape from it. I even savoured it with the desperate enjoyment of the sick man who scratches his sores and laughs to see blood on his nail.

I was seized by a nameless rage against life, against man, against everything. In my heart were treasures of tenderness, and I became more ferocious than the tiger. I longed to annihilate creation, to sleep with it in the infinity of Nothing. Why did I not wake by the glare of blazing cities! I longed to hear the shudder of bone crackling in the flame, to cross rivers turgid with corpses, to gallop down bowed peoples and crush them under the four hooves of my horse; to be Genghis Khan, Tamerlane, Nero—to terrify the world with my frown.

In proportion to the ecstasies and exaltations I had known, I withdrew into myself and suffered. For a long time now my heart has been arid, no new thing may enter it, and it is as empty as the tombs in which the dead have rotted away. I held the sun in hatred, I was infuriated by the murmur of the river, by the prospect of the woods, nothing seemed so futile as the country. Everything grew sombre and stale, and I lived in a perpetual twilight.

Sometimes I asked myself whether I were not wrong. I reviewed my youth, my future: but how pitiful a youth, how empty a future!

When I wished to leave the spectacle of my own misery

and look at the world, all that I could discover were screams, cries, tears, convulsions: the same play perpetually repeated with the same actors. And there are people, I said to myself, who study all that and return to the task each morning! Nothing but a great love could have extricated me, but I looked on that as something which is not of this world, and I regretted bitterly the lack of all the happiness I had dreamed.

Death then seemed beautiful. I have loved it always: as a child, I desired it merely from curiosity to know what is in the tombs, what dreams are in that sleep. I remember that I often used to scrape the verdigris from old pennies to poison myself with it, tried to swallow pins, walked close to garret windows to throw myself into the street. When I reflect that almost all children seek, like me, suicide in their games, shall I not conclude that man, whatever he may say, loves death with an avid devotion? It gives him all that he creates, he comes from it and returns to it, he thinks of it as long as he lives, he has the germ of it in his body, the desire for it in his heart.

It is so sweet to imagine that you are no more! A graveyard is so tranquil! There, as you lie stiff, wrapped in your shroud, your arms crossed on your breast, the centuries go by, waking you no more than the wind passing over the grass. Many a time have I gazed on the long stone statues lying on their tombs in cathedral chapels. Their calm is more profound than any offered

48

by this life. The smile on their cold lips seems to have come from the depths of the tomb, and you would say that they are asleep, that they are savouring death. To have no more need of tears, to feel no more those sudden emptinesses when everything seems to crumble beneath you like a rotten scaffolding, is happiness above all happinesses, joy without morrow, dream without waking. And then one goes perhaps to a more beautiful world beyond the stars, where one lives a life of light and perfume, where one is perhaps some essence of the fragrance of the rose, the freshness of the meadow. But no! Ah, no! I would rather think that one is quite dead, that nothing issues from the coffin; and, if one still must feel something, let it be one's own non-being, let death gloat on death, admire itself; let one have just enough life to feel that one is no more alive.

I climbed to the top of towers, I hung over the abyss and waited the coming of vertigo. I had an unutterable desire to fling myself down, to float through the air, to scatter myself on the winds. I used to eye dagger points, pistol muzzles, put them to my forehead, accustom myself to the feel of the coldness and sharpness of their contact. Sometimes I watched carters swing around street corners, and as I saw the great wide wheels grind the dust on the cobbles I imagined my head being thoroughly crushed beneath them as the horses plodded ahead. But I never wished to be buried, for the coffin terrifies me; I would rather lie on a bed of dead leaves in the depths of the woods and let my body be dispersed little by little beneath the birds' beaks and the storm rain.

In Paris one day I stood for a long time on the Pont Neuf. It was winter. The Seine drifted great round floes slowly down on the current, they crashed together under the arches; the river was green. And I thought of those who had come there to finish it all. How many had passed the place where I was standing, hurrying to their loves or their business with head erect, to return one day with dragging steps, shivering at the approach of death! They neared the parapet, climbed on to it, leaped. What misery has ended here, what happiness begun! The cold, the damp of that grave! It gapes, it gapes; and how many has it engulfed! They are all there, rolling slowly along the bed, their faces distorted, their limbs blue; each of these icy waves rolls them on in their sleep, carries them softly towards the sea.

Sometimes old men looked at me enviously and told me that I was lucky to be young, that youth was the good age. Their hollow eyes admired my unlined brow and they recalled their loves and told me of them; but I often asked myself whether life had been better in their time, and as I saw nothing in myself to envy, I was jealous of their regrets because they concealed happinesses I had not had. And then there came childish weaknesses that were pitiable; I used to laugh softly and almost for no cause, like a convalescent. Sometimes I was seized by an access of tenderness for my dog and would hug him passionately; or I would rediscover some old school clothes in a closet and dream of the day I first wore them and of the places they had been with me, and I would lose myself in memories of all the days I had lived. For memories are sweet, no matter whether sad or gay, and the saddest are yet the most delightful, for they do not epitomize the Infinite? Sometimes one spends centuries thinking of a certain hour that will not return; it has passed into non-existence for ever, and you would buy it back with your whole future.

But such memories are candles dispersed through a great dark room; they shine amid the dimness, only their radiance is to be seen; things near them stand out bright while all the rest is the blacker, the more wrapped in shadows and gloom.

Before I go further, I must relate this incident:

I do not remember the exact year, but it was during the holidays. I woke up in a good mood and looked out the window. Day was at hand. The moon stood pale in the sky. Grey and rosy mists steamed softly between the clefts in the hills and melted into the air. The hens were cackling in the farmyard below. I heard a cart go down the road behind the house which leads to the fields, its wheels rumbling in the ruts. The haymakers were going to work. There was dew on the hedge and the sun shone on it. There was a scent of water and grass.

I went out and away towards X. . . . ; I had three leagues to walk. I set out quite alone, with neither stick nor dog. At first I went by the paths that wind among the corn. I passed beneath apple trees and along hedges. I thought of nothing, listened to the noise of my steps; and the cadence of my movements lulled thought. I was free and silent and tranquil. It was hot. From time to time I stopped, for my temples were beating. Crickets were chirping in the stubble. I went on. I passed through a hamlet and saw not a soul, the yards were all silent: it was a Sunday, I think. The cows lay in the grass in the shade of the trees and calmly ruminated, twitching their ears to keep off the flies. I remember walking down a road; there was a pebbly brook, and green lizards and insects with golden wings were climbing slowly up the road-banks—it was a sunken lane, covered with leafage.

I found myself on an upland, in a reaped field. The sea lay before me, deep blue; the glint of the sun upon it was like a profusion of luminous beads, and the waves were furrowed with lines of fire. The horizon glowed and blazed between the azure sky and the darker sea, and the arc of the sky rose above my head and curved down behind the waves which mounted to meet it, forming the circle of an invisible infinity. I lay in a furrow and stared at the sky, lost in the contemplation of its beauty.

It was a cornfield in which I was lying. I could hear quail fluttering around me and settling on the clods of earth. The sea was calm, and it murmured, a sigh rather than a voice. The sun itself seemed to have its sound; it flooded everything, its rays scorched my limbs, and the earth filled me with its own heat. I was drowned in light, and when I shut my eyes, the light persisted. The tang of the waves rose up to me with the smell of kelp and seaweed. At times the waves seemed to cease or to die away noiselessly on the foam-rimmed shore, like a sound-less kiss. Then, when the swelling ocean was silent in the pause between two waves, for an instant I heard quail calling, then the sound of the sea began again, and, after it, that of the birds.

I ran down to the shore across tracts of boulders over which I leapt sure-footed. Proudly I flung back my head, proudly I breathed in the fresh breeze which dried the sweat in my hair. The spirit of God filled me and I felt my heart expand, I had a strange emotion of adoration. I longed to be absorbed into the sun's light and lose myself in that azure immensity along with the salt smell that rose from the crests of the waves. And then I was seized by a lunatic joy and began to walk as if all the joys of heaven had entered my soul. The cliff projected at that point in such a way that the whole coast vanished and I could see nothing but the sea. The waves rolled up the shingle to my feet, foamed on the rocks at water-level, broke on them in cadence, embraced them like watery arms, like lucent veils, and fell back transfused with blue. The wind blew the spume around me and wrinkled the surface of the pools left behind in the crevices; the sea-weed swayed and dripped, still rocked by the motion of the retreating wave. From time to time a gull flew past with great sweeps of its wings and rose to the very top of the cliffs. As the sea retreated and its sound grew more distant, like a dying refrain, the beach advanced towards me, discovering the furrows traced by waves on the sand. And then I understood all the happiness of creation, all the joy with which God has endowed it for man. I thought that Nature was as beautiful as some perfect harmony audible to ecstasy alone. Something as tender as love, as pure as prayer, rose up for me from the depths of the horizon and fell from the summits of the riven cliffs, from the heights of the sky; the sound of the ocean and the light of the day combined to form something exquisite that I took possession of as of a celestial domain; I felt that I was dwelling in it, happy and noble as the eagle that gazes on the sun and mounts its beams.

Then all on earth seemed beautiful, nothing inharmonious or evil. I loved everything, even the stones that tired my feet, the hard rocks I grasped with my hands, even insensible Nature, which I could imagine hearing and loving me; and I thought how sweet it was to sing canticles kneeling at evening at the feet of a madonna in the light of candles, and to love the Virgin Mary, who appears to sailors in a corner of the sky, holding the sweet Jesus Child in her arms.

Then it ended. Soon enough I remembered that I had

to go on living. I came to myself, and began to walk, feeling that the curse had resumed its sway, that I was returning to humanity. Life had come back as it comes back to frozen limbs: by the sensation of pain; and as my happiness had been unutterable, the discouragement into which I now fell was unspeakable too. I went on to X. . . .

I returned home that evening. I passed by the same way, I saw the prints of my feet in the sand, and the place where I had lain in the grass; and it seemed all a dream. There are days on which one lives through two existences, the second no more than a recollection of the first; and I often stopped before a thicket, a tree, the corner of a road, as if some event of my life had happened there that morning.

It was almost night when I reached home. The doors were shut. The dogs began to bark.

*   *   *

The ideas of pleasure and love which had assailed me when I was fifteen returned at eighteen. If you have understood something of what has been related above, you will recall that I was still virgin at that age and I had not yet been in love. As concerned the beauty and the clamour of the passions, the poets were furnishing themes to my meditation; and as for the pleasures of the senses, the enjoyments of the body coveted by adolescents, I was nourishing an incessant desire for them in my heart by exciting my mind in every way I could. Just as lovers try to exhaust their love by giving themselves over to it without respite and hope to rid themselves of it by dreaming it out, so I believed that my thinking alone would exhaust the subject, that in this way I would empty the cup of temptation by drinking. But, returning always to the point from which I had started, I revolved in an inevitable circle; in vain I beat my head against it, in a longing for greater freedom. By night, I must have had the most beautiful dreams one can dream, for in the morning my heart was filled with smiles and delicious agitation; waking angered me, and I awaited impatiently the return of sleep to restore to me the quivering delights of which I thought all day. I could have experienced them in actuality at any moment, but they filled me with a kind of religious terror.

It was then that I felt the demon of the flesh come to life in every muscle of my body, race through all my blood. I pitied the ingenuous age when I trembled before a woman's glance, when I swooned before pictures and statues. I wanted to live, enjoy, love! I felt dimly the oncoming of my season of heat, as a glow of summer is wafted to you on the warm winds of the first sunny days, although neither grass nor leaves nor roses have yet appeared. What are you to do? Whom are you to love? Who is to love you? What great lady will you please? What superhuman beauty will open her arms to you? Who shall tell of all the sad walks by the banks of lonely streams, all the sighs addressed to the stars by swelling hearts on hot nights when breasts are full to choking!

To dream of love is to dream of all, the infinite in happiness, the mystery of joy. How ardently our gaze devours you, how intensely it lights upon your head, oh you lovely and triumphant women! Your every movement breathes grace and corruption, there are melodies in the folds of your dress which move us to our depths, and from all your body there flows a something which ravishes and kills us.

There was one word which seemed to me the most beautiful of all human words: adultery. It is vaguely enveloped with an exquisite sweetness, it is fragrant with a peculiar magic. Every story that is told, every book read, every gesture made, speaks it, makes commentary on it eternally for the young man's heart; he drugs himself wantonly with it, finds in it a supreme poetry, compounded of delight and blasphemy.

It was at the approach of spring, when the lilac begins to blossom and the birds sing beneath the first leaves, that I most felt the longing in my heart for love, to melt utterly in love, to be absorbed into some great sweet emotion, to gain new life, as it were, from the very light and scents. For a few hours every year I still find in myself a virginity which is reborn with the buds; but joy does not flower again with the roses, and now there is no more green in my heart than there is on the highroad where the scorching wind wearies the eyes and the dust rises in whirling clouds.

However, now that I am on the point of telling you the sequel, of returning to this memory, I tremble and hesitate. It is as if I were going to revisit a mistress of long ago. With sinking heart, one stops on every step of her staircase: one fears meeting her again and fears lest she be absent. It is the same with certain ideas with which one has lived too long: one would like to rid oneself of them for ever, yet they pulse in you like life itself and in them the heart breathes its natural atmosphere.

I have told you that I loved the sun. On the days when it shone, my heart used to have something of the serenity of radiant horizons, something of the loftiness of the sky. It was summer . . . ah! the pen cannot express it! . . . and it was hot. I went out and no one at home knew that I had gone. There were few people in the streets. The pavement was dry, and from time to time warm gusts rose from beneath the ground and went to one's head; the walls of the houses gave off lambent reflections and the shade itself seemed more glowing than light. Swarms of flies buzzed over the dung at the street corners, circling in the sunbeams like a great golden wheel. The sloping roofs were silhouetted in straight lines against the blue of the sky; the stone of the buildings was dark, and there were no birds around the belfries.

I walked on, seeking rest, longing for a breeze, something to lift me off the earth, sweep me off in a whirlwind.

I left the suburbs behind and found myself passing behind gardens on ways that were half road, half footpath. The foliage of the trees was pierced here and there by glancing sunbeams; the blades of the grass stood upright in the masses of shade; pebble points shot rays, the dust crunched beneath my feet, all nature was corrosive. At last the sun was hidden; a heavy cloud came up as though presaging storm. The torment I had suffered all that day changed its nature: I was no longer harassed but oppressed, no longer racked but stifled.

I lay face downward on the ground in a place where there seemed to be the most shade, silence and darkness, the place that might best conceal me; and, panting, I plunged into unbridled desire. The clouds hung heavy and sultry, they weighed on me, they crushed me as one breast crushes another. I felt a need for sensual pleasure, a need headier than the perfume of the clematis, more searing than the sun on the garden wall. Ah! why had I nothing to press in my arms, to stifle in the warmth of my embrace; or, better, why could I not become two beings, that I might love this other, melt into it, become one with it? This was no longer the desire for some dim ideal nor the longing for a lovely, vanished dream; like a river that has left its bed, my passion overflowed on all sides, cutting furious ravines; it flooded my heart and made it resound with a thousand madnesses and tumults that were wilder than mountain torrents.

59

I went to the river bank. I have always loved water and the gentle motion of the ripples. Peace reigned: the white water-lilies shivered in the murmur of the current, the waves rolled slowly on, one overlapping the other. The islands in midstream dipped their green heads to the water, the banks smiled, and nothing was to be heard but the voice of the stream.

There were several great trees near by, and the coolness of the conjunction of water and shade was so delectable that I felt myself smile. Just as the muse that is in us dilates her nostrils when she hears some harmony and breathes in the lovely sound, so something in me dilated to inhale a universal joy; as I gazed at the clouds rolling by in the sky, at the velvet sward of the bank striped yellow in the rays of the sun, and as I listened to the rippling of the water and the rustling of the tree-tops, although there was not a breath of wind, there, solitary, tranquil and yet troubled, I felt myself swooning with bliss beneath the weight of this amorous nature—and I called to Love! My lips trembled and went out as if I had scented the breath of some other mouth, my hands reached for something to fondle, my eyes strained to discover in the curve of every wave, in the contour of every swelling cloud, some form, some delight, some revelation; desire breathed from my every pore, and my heart was tender and full of a contained harmony. I shook my hair about my head, let it cover my face, and took pleasure in breathing the smell of it. I stretched myself on the moss at the foot of the trees and longed for more languorous languors—I longed to be smothered beneath roses, to be martyred by kisses; to be the flower shaken by the wind, the bank washed by the stream, the earth fertilized by the sun.

The grass was soft to walk on, and I walked; each step brought renewed pleasure and I enjoyed the softness of the turf underfoot. The distant meadows teemed with animals, horses and foals, and the horizon rang with neighings and the clatter of hooves. The downs rose and fell in wide, gentle waves as they sloped from the hills; the river wound serpentine, vanished behind the islands, reappeared between grass and reeds. All was beautiful, seemed happy, pursued its law, its natural course: I alone was sick, with an agony of desire.

All at once I took to flight: back to the city, across the bridges, down the streets, over the squares I fled. Women brushed by me, and there were many of them, walking quickly, and they were all marvellously beautiful. Never had I gazed so straight into their shining eyes, never had I observed so closely the antelope lightness of their walk. Duchesses leaning from emblazoned coaches seemed to smile on me, to invite me to silken love; ladies in wraps bent from their balconies to see me and gazed at me, saying: "Love us! Love us!" They urged their love on me, as I well saw in their pose, in their eyes, even in their very immobility! There was Woman everywhere: I rubbed elbows with her, I brushed against her, I inhaled

Woman, for the air was redolent of her fragrance; I saw the pearly moisture on her neck between the folds of her shawl, the plumes nodding on her hat as she walked, the dress lifted by her heel as she passed in front of me. When I came near, her gloved hand made a movement. Not this woman nor that one, one no more than the other, but all of them, each of them, in the infinite variety of their forms and of my corresponding desire—however they might be clothed, I adorned them with a magnificent nudity on which I feasted my eyes; and passing so close to them, I quickly carried away my fill of voluptuous thoughts, aphrodisiac perfumes, exciting contacts, alluring forms.

I knew well enough where I was going: to a house in a little street through which I often used to pass to feel my heart beat quicker; it had green shutters and there were three steps to climb—oh, I knew it by heart, I had stared at it long enough, turning aside out of my way merely to see those shut windows. When I came to the street at last, after I had walked for a century, I thought I should choke. There was no one in sight. I crept forward, forward. I can still feel the door pressing against my shoulder—it yielded; I had feared that it might have been cemented into the wall—but no, it swung on a hinge, softly, without a sound.

I climbed a staircase. The stairs were dark, the steps were worn and rocked beneath my tread. I went up and up; I could see nothing, hear nothing, no one spoke to me, I could not breathe. Finally I entered a room. It seemed to me to be vast—the impression was due to its dimness: the windows were open, but great yellow curtains hung to the floor and shut out the daylight, so that the room was full of a tint of tarnished gold. A woman was seated at the window on the right at the far end. She could not have heard me, for she did not turn as I entered. I stood still, gazing at her, rapt.

She was wearing a white dress with short sleeves. She sat with her elbow on the windowsill, one hand beside her mouth, seeming to gaze at something vague and indistinct below. Her black hair, braided and plaited on her temples, glistened like a raven's wing; her head was bent a little, and some little black curls, escaping from the rest, twined on her neck. Her great curving golden comb was decorated with beads of red coral.

She cried out when she saw me and leapt to her feet. At first I was dazzled by the brilliance of her two great eyes; when at last I was able to raise mine from beneath the weight of that gaze, I saw a face of ravishing loveliness. A single straight line, beginning at the crown of her head, passed along the parting of her hair, down between her great arching eyebrows, along her aquiline nose with its dilated, lifted nostrils like those in an antique cameo, divided her warm upper lip shadowed with blue down, and continued on down to her neck—her neck that was full, white and round. Through her thin dress I saw the

63

shape of her breasts come and go in the motion of her breathing. She stood facing me there, bathed in the sunlight that passed through the yellow curtains and set off yet more the white dress and the dark hair.

At length she smiled, almost pityingly, almost tenderly, and I approached. I do not know what she had put on her hair, but it had a scent that made my heart soften and melt like a peach beneath the tongue. She said: "What is it? Come!"

She sat down on a long grey-covered sofa standing against the wall. I sat beside her. She took my hand; hers was warm, and we sat looking long at each other, and we did not speak.

Never had I seen a woman so close. All her beauty enveloped me; her arm lay against mine, the folds of her dress fell over my legs, the warmth of her thigh seared me; in this proximity I felt the undulation of her whole body. I gazed at the curve of her shoulder, the blue veins of her temple. She said: "Well!"

"Well!" I replied with seeming gaiety, for I wished to shake off the fascination that was lulling my senses.

But I said no more: I was rapt in contemplation of her. Without a word, she put her arm around me and drew me down to her in a mute embrace. I held her in my arms, I pressed my mouth to her shoulder, and blissfully drank in the first kiss of love; I savoured in it all the long desire of my youth, the new-found realization of all my dreams of voluptuous pleasure. Then I flung back my head the better to gaze on her face. Her eyes shone, set me aflame; even more than her arms her eyes embraced me, I was utterly lost in their depths. Our fingers were intertwined; hers were long and delicate and moved in my hand with subtle and intricate caresses; with the slightest effort I could have crushed them; I pressed them, to feel them the more.

I cannot recall what she said to me nor what I replied. I lay there long, lost, tense, swaying to the beating of my heart. Each minute increased my intoxication, each minute some new sensation assailed my soul; my whole body quivered with impatience, with desire, with joy: yet I was grave, more sombre than gay, serious, absorbed as though in something divine and supreme. She pressed my head to her heart, but gently, as if she were afraid of crushing me to her.

With a movement of her shoulder, she slipped her arm from her sleeve; her dress fell away, she wore no corset, her shift lay open wide. She had one of those splendid bosoms on which one would wish to die, stifled by love. As she sat on my knee, her pose was that of a simple, dreamy child, and her lovely profile was cut in the purest lines. The fold of the ravishing curve beneath her armpit was the smile of her shoulder. Her white back drooped a little, as if she were a little weary, and her falling dress sank in broad billows to the floor. She lifted her eyes and hummed a sad, languorous refrain.

I took her comb, drew it out: her hair unrolled like a wave, and the long black tresses fell billowing to her waist. I passed my hands over it, and in it, and beneath it; I plunged my arms, my face into it in ecstasy. Now I took pleasure in dividing it in two behind her and bringing it in front to veil her breasts, now I would gather it all up together and pull it down to watch her head go back and her soft neck thrust forward. She was as passive under this as if she had been dead.

Suddenly she released herself, freed her feet from the dress, and leapt into the bed with the agility of a cat; the mattress gave beneath her feet, the bed creaked. She flung back the curtains abruptly, then lay back. She stretched out her arms to me, she held me to her. Oh, the very bedclothes seemed still warmed by the passionate caresses that had been exchanged there.

Her moist soft hand moved over my body, she kissed my face, my mouth, my eyes, and each of her urgent caresses made me swoon. She stretched herself on her back, and she sighed. Now she half-closed her eyes and looked at me with a voluptuous irony, now she rose on her elbow, twisted around, kicked her heels in the air; she was full of charming playfulnesses, of movements at once ingenuous and sophisticated. At length, abandoning herself to me completely, she lifted her eyes to heaven and gave a great sigh that shook her whole body.... Her warm, tremulous flesh stretched beneath me, quivering. From head to foot I was all sensuality; my mouth pressed to

66

hers, our fingers intertwined, shaken by one spasm, interlaced in one embrace. Breathing the scent of her hair, the breath of her lips, I felt myself die a delicious death. I delayed for a few moments longer, savouring the racing of my heart, the last tremors of my nerves: then everything seemed to go dark, to vanish.

She too said nothing. Motionless as a statue of flesh, her abundant black hair framing her white face, she lay there with her arms loosely and languidly outstretched. From time to time a convulsive tremor shook her knees and hips. Red traces of my kisses still burned on her breast. A hoarse, complaining sound came from her throat, like the sound of one asleep after much weeping and sobbing. Suddenly I heard her murmur: "What if you forgot yourself and became a mother!" I remember nothing more of what followed. She crossed her legs one over the other and rocked from side to side as though she were in a hammock.

She passed her hand through my hair as if she were playing with a child, and asked me if I had had a mistress. I answered, Yes; and as she was going on, I added that she was beautiful and married. She asked me other questions: about my name, my life, my family.

"And you," I asked her, "have you loved?"

"Loved? No!" And she broke into a forced laugh that disconcerted me.

She asked me again whether my mistress was beautiful, and, after a silence, added: "Oh, how

67

she must love you! Tell me your name, yes? Your name!"

I asked her hers in return.

"Marie," she replied, "but I had another, that is not what I was called at home."

And now I recall no more; it is all gone, it was so long ago! There are certain things, however, which I can still see as clearly as if it were yesterday; her room, for example. I see the bedspread, worn in the centre, the mahogany bed with its bronze ornaments and curtains of red moiré silk that crackled under one's fingers—their fringes were worn. Two vases of artificial flowers on the mantelpiece, and the clock with its face borne on four alabaster columns; here and there on the wall an old engraving in a dark wood frame, depicting women bathing, harvesters, fishermen.

And she! She! Sometimes the memory of her comes back to me so vivid and so precise that I see anew every detail of her face with that astonishing fidelity of memory that dreams alone give us, when we see again friends who have been dead for years, wearing the same clothes, speaking with the same voice, so that we are terrified. I well remember that she had a beauty spot on her lower lip on the left, which became visible in a dimple of her skin when she smiled. She had lost her freshness, and the corners of her mouth were drawn, in a way that told of bitterness and weariness.

When I was ready to leave, she said goodbye.

68

"Goodbye!"
"Shall I see you again?"
"Perhaps!"

I went out. The air revived me, and I felt utterly changed; I thought that no one could have helped noticing in my face that I was no longer the same man. I walked lightly, proudly, content and free. I had nothing more to learn, nothing more to experience, nothing more to desire from life. I returned home. An eternity had passed since I had left it. I went up to my room and sat down on my bed, overwhelmed by my whole day, which weighed on me with incredible pressure. It was perhaps seven o'clock in the evening; the sun was setting, the sky was on fire, the glowing horizon flamed above the roofs of the houses. The garden was already in shadow and full of sadness; red and orange rings wheeled in the corners of the walls and sank and rose in the bushes, and the ground was grey and dry. In the street some of the common people, on the arms of their women, were singing as they passed on their way to the outdoor cafés beyond the city gates.

I went over and over what I had done, and I fell into an indefinable melancholy. I was full of disgust, satiated, weary. "But this very morning," I said to myself, "I didn't feel this way; I was fresher, happier—why should that be?" And in imagination I went over all the streets I had walked, all the women I had met, all the paths I had traversed; I returned to Marie and lingered over every detail of my recollection, I pressed my memory to make it yield me all that it possibly could. Thus I spent my whole evening. Night came, and, like an old man, I remained bound up in this absorbing meditation. I felt that I would recapture nothing; that other loves might come but they would not resemble this one; the first fragrance had been tasted, the melody had fled, and I desired my desire and I missed my enjoyment.

When I considered my past and my present life, that is to say, the anticipations of the days that were gone and the apathy that now overwhelmed me, I no longer knew in what corner of my being my heart was to be found: whether I was dreaming or acting, whether I was full of disgust or of desire, for I experienced at the same time the nausea of satiety and the ardour of hope.

So Love was no more than that! So Woman was no more than that! Why, in God's name, are we still hungry after we have had our fill? Why have we such aspirations and such disappointments? Why is the heart of man so large and life so small? There are days when the love of the very angels could not satisfy him, and he wearies in an hour of all the caresses on earth.

But vanished illusion leaves us its fairy scent, and we seek traces of it on all the paths down which it has fled; we cherish the thought that all is not over so soon, that life is only beginning, that a world is opening before us. Can we have really expended dreams so sublime, desires so fiery, to end in no more than this? I refused to renounce all the beautiful things I had forged for myself. Before the loss of my virginity, I had created for myself other forms, vaguer but lovelier—other delights, less precise, like the desire I had for them, but heavenly and infinite. With the images I had once conjured and now compelled myself to call up again mingled the intense recollection of my latest sensations, and the whole, phantom and body, dream and reality, melting into one, the woman I had just left became a synthetic figure in which my whole past was concentrated and from which all my future took its origin. As I thought of her in my solitude, I observed her again from every angle, tried to discover in her something more, something I had not perceived, something I had not discovered that first time. The desire to see her again seized me, possessed me; it was a fatality that drew me, a slope down which I was sliding.

A lovely night! It was hot; I was bathed in sweat when I arrived at her door. There was a light in her window: no doubt she was still awake. I stopped. I was afraid, and I waited there a long time, uncertain what to do, filled with a thousand agitated indecisions. Once again I went in, once again I slid my hand by the banister of her staircase, once again I turned her key.

She was alone, as she had been that morning; she was sitting in the same place, almost in the same posture, but she had changed her dress; now it was black. The lace edging the neck trembled on her white throat; her skin

71

glistened, her face had the lascivious pallor that comes from candlelight. With half-closed lips, hair loosely spread over her shoulders, eyes raised to the heavens, she seemed to be searching for some vanished star.

With a swift joyous bound she rushed to me and pressed me in her arms. It was, for us, one of those quivering embraces that lovers must exchange at their meetings, when, after long peering through the dark, listening to every sound of footsteps in the leaves, watching every dim form that passes through the glade, they are together at last and hold each other tight.

She said to me—and her voice was both urgent and gentle at once: "Ah, do you love me, that you come back to me? Tell me, speak, my sweetheart, do you love me?" Her voice was penetrating yet mellow, like the highest range of a flute.

Sinking to her knees, half-swooning, she held me in her arms and gazed at me with a sombre intoxication. And I, although I was astonished by this sudden access of passion, was charmed, was exalted, by it.

The satin of her dress crackled beneath my fingers with the sound of sparks. At moments, after feeling the velvety material, I felt the warm softness of her bare arm; her dress seemed a very part of her and breathed the seduction of the most gorgeous nakedness.

She absolutely insisted on sitting on my knee, and began her usual caress, passing her hand through my hair while she gazed fixedly into my face, her eyes plunged into mine. As she sat motionless, her pupils seemed to dilate, and from them issued a subtle fluid that I felt running over my heart. Every effluvium of that gaze, like one of the successive circles described by the osprey, bound me ever more tightly to that terrible magic.

"Ah, you do love me," she cried, "you do love me, for you have come back to me, for me! But what is it—you are sad, you do not speak? Do you want me no more?" She paused, then continued: "How beautiful you are, my angel! You are as beautiful as the day! Kiss me, ah, love me! A kiss, quick, a kiss!"

She hung on my lips, she cooed like a dove, her breast swelled with the sigh she drew from its depths. "All night, yes? All night, the whole night, for us two? Oh, if I could have a lover like you, a lover young and eager who would love me well and think of me only! Ah, how I should love him!" And she excited my desire in a way that made me feel that God had come down from his heaven.

"But have you no lover?" I asked.

"Who? I? Is love for women like us? Who thinks of us? Who wants us? Us? Even you, will you remember me tomorrow? Perhaps you will say to yourself, 'Oh yes, I slept with a wench last night'—but, well . . ." And she began to hum and to dance, hands on her hips, with obscene movements. "How is that for dancing? Wait, look at my costume."

She opened her closet, and on a shelf I saw a black

mask and some blue ribbons with a domino, and there was also a pair of black velvet knickers with gold braid stripes hanging on a hook, tawdry relics of the last carnival. "My poor costume," she said, "how many balls I've worn it to! I danced so much last winter."

The window was open. The candle flickered in the wind, and she took it from the mantelpiece and set it on the bedtable. She sat down on the bed and sank into profound reflection, head bowed on breast. Nor did I speak. I waited. The warm scent of the August night rose up to us; we could hear the rustling of the trees on the boulevard, the swaying of the window curtains. All that night there was thunder in the air; often I caught a glimpse of her pallid face, contracted with an expression of passionate sadness, in a flash of lightning. Clouds raced by; the moon, half-hidden by them, shone out at times in a bit of clear sky.

She undressed slowly, with the regular movements of a machine. When she was in her shift, she came over to me, barefoot took me by the hand, and led me to her bed. She did not look at me, her thoughts were elsewhere. Her lips were pink and moist, her nostrils wide, her eyes afire; she seemed to vibrate beneath the pressure of her thoughts, as a resonant instrument, even after the artist is gone, sometimes gives out a secret fragrance of sleeping chords.

Lying beside me, she displayed, with the pride of the courtesan, all the splendours of her flesh. I saw her firm

74

naked bosom, swelling as if with a continual stormy
murmur, her pearly bare belly with its deep-hollowed
navel, that quivering, elastic belly, so soft that one would
plunge one's head into it as into a pillow of warm satin.
Her hips were superb, true woman's hips, with those
lines that as they merge into rounded thighs always evoke
the subtle and corrupt form of something serpentine,
demoniac. Her skin, moistened by sweat, was cool and
cleaving. In the dark her eyes shone with a terrible gleam.
The amber bracelet she wore on her right arm rang when
she clutched at the wainscoting of the alcove. Once during those hours she cried, as she pressed my head to her
heart: "Where did you come from, oh angel of love, of
desire, of delight? Who was your mother? What were
her thoughts when she conceived you? Did she dream of
the strength of African lions? Or the perfume of those
trees in far-off lands, so fragrant that one dies at their
scent? You say nothing? Look at me with your great
eyes, look at me, look at me! Give me your mouth! Your
mouth! Here, here, here is mine!"

Here teeth chattered as if with great cold, her parted
lips quivered and gave forth frantic words: "Ah, I would
be jealous of you if we were lovers! The least woman that
looked at you . . ." Her words ended in a cry. And at other
moments she held me fast with rigid arms, and said very
softly that she would die.

"Ah, how beautiful is a man when he is young! If I
were a man, all the women would love me; my eyes

would shine so seductively, I should be so well dressed, so handsome! Your mistress loves you, yes? I should like to know her. How do you see each other? At your house or hers? Or is it in the park as you ride past? You must look so well on horseback! Or at the theatre when the play is over and you help her into her cloak? Or at night in her garden? What lovely hours you must spend talking together on the bench beneath the arbour!"

I let her talk on, for it seemed to me that she was creating an ideal mistress for me, and I fell in love with this phantom newly presented to my imagination, which gleamed there more fleeting than a will-o'-the-wisp on a country evening.

"Have you known each other long? Tell me something about her. What kind of things do you do for her? Is she tall or short? Does she sing?"

I could not help undeceiving her. I even told her of my apprehensions in coming to see her, of the remorse, or, rather, the strange fear I had felt afterwards, and the sudden reaction that had driven me back to her. When I assured her that I had never had a mistress, that I had looked everywhere for one, and that she was the first to accept my embraces, she drew near me in amazement and grasped my arm as if I were an illusion she wanted to seize.

"Is it true?" she cried. "Oh, don't lie to me! You are a virgin and I have deflowered you, my poor angel? Somehow your kisses did have an innocence about them

—like a child's, if children made love. But you amaze me! You are enchanting. The more I look at you, the more I love you. Your cheeks are as soft as a peach, your skin is white, white, your lovely hair is strong and thick. Ah, how I would love you if you would let me! I have never seen anyone like you. Your look might be merely a look of kindness, and yet your eyes are burning me, and I want to be close to you and press you to me!"

They were the first words of love I had heard in my life. Wherever they come from, our heart accepts them happily and tremulously. Remember that, reader! I drank deep of them. How I revelled in this new heaven!

"Yes, yes, kiss me, kiss me deep! Your kisses make me young again!" she cried. "I love to breathe the scent of you, like the scent of my honeysuckle in June—so sweet and so fresh. Your teeth—show me—they're whiter than mine—I am not so beautiful as you—ah, but this is delight!"

And she pressed her mouth to my neck, exploring it with avid kisses, as a beast of prey explores the belly of its victim.

"What has come over me tonight? You have set me on fire—I want to drink and dance and sing. Have you ever wanted to be a little bird? We could fly away together. It must be so sweet to make love in the air; the winds carrying you along, the clouds all round you. . . . No, lie quiet and let me look at you, let me look long at you so that I can always remember you!"

"Why?"

"Why!" she replied. "To remember you, to think of you. I'll think of you at night when I don't sleep and at morning when I wake; I'll think of you all day as I sit at my window watching people pass; but most of all I'll think of you in the evening, when it has grown too dark to see anything but the candles are not yet lit; I'll remember your face, your body, your lovely body that breathes out delight, and your voice!—Oh, listen, my love, let me cut some of your hair; I'll put it in this bracelet, and it will never leave me."

She got up at once, took her scissors, and cut a lock of hair from the back of my head. They were little pointed scissors, and they squeaked on their pin. I still feel on the back of my neck the coldness of the steel and the touch of Marie's hand.

Hair given and exchanged is one of lovers' happiest inventions. How many beautiful hands, since nights first began, have passed gifts of black tresses through the grilles of balconies! Away with your watch chains in figure-of-eight twists, your encircled rings, your lockets with their clover-leaf designs, away with all hair polluted by the vulgar hand of the barber. I would have it quite simply knotted at either end with a thread, for fear of losing a single hair; and the locks should be cut by oneself from the beloved head at some supreme moment, the culminating moment of a first love, or on the eve of parting. Ah, hair! The magnificent mantle of woman in primitive days, when it reached to her heels and hid her arms as she walked beside her man on the banks of great rivers, and the first breezes of creation stirred at once the fronds of the palm, the mane of the lion and the hair of woman! I love hair! How often have I gazed on it in spaded earth, amid yellowing bones and pieces of rotting wood, in graveyards that were being dug up, or in old churches being demolished! Often the sun cast a pale glint on it and made it glisten like threads of gold. I loved to think of the days when some hand now dry caressed it and spread it out on the pillow when it was still growing thickly on some white scalp oily with liquid perfume, when some mouth, toothless now, gathered and kissed it and bit its ends with sobs of bliss.

I let her cut mine, with a childish vanity. I was ashamed to ask for some of hers in return, and I regret it now that I have nothing, not a glove, not a ribbon, not so much as three dried rose leaves preserved in a book, nothing but the memory of the love of a common whore.

When she had finished, she came back and lay down again beside me. Trembling with delight, she crept beneath the covers; she shivered and made herself small like a child; at length she fell asleep, her head pillowed on my breast.

Each time I breathed, I felt the weight of the sleeping head lift over my heart. What intimate communion did I share with this unknown being? We had been unaware of one another before that day; chance had brought us

79

together, and there we were in the same bed, united by some nameless power; and we were to part, never to meet again. The motes that race and fly in the air have meetings that last longer than those of loving hearts on earth. Each night solitary desires and dreams take off and set out in search of company: one soul sighs perhaps after the unknown soul which is sighing after it in another hemisphere, beneath another sky.

What dreams were passing through that head? Was she thinking of her family, of her first lover, of the world, of men, of some rich life lit with luxury, of some longed-for love?—of me, perhaps! I fastened my gaze on her pale brow, I spied on her sleep, I tried to discover some meaning in the hoarse sound that came from her nostrils.

It was raining. I listened to the sounds of the rain and of Marie's sleep. The candles were about to go out, flickering in the crystal sconces. The dawn began to show; a line of yellow appeared in the sky, spread horizontally, took on more and more tints of gold and wine; the darkness of the room was infiltrated by a feeble pallid light tinged with violet, which dimmed the shimmer of the expiring candles and their reflections in the mirror.

As Marie lay thus stretched upon me, certain portions of her body caught the light, others were in shadow. She had shifted a little, and her head was lower than her breasts. Her right arm, the one on which she wore the bracelet, hung out of the bed and almost touched the floor. There was a bouquet of violets in a glass of water on the bedtable. I stretched out my hand, took the flowers, broke the thread with my teeth, and smelled them. The heat of the previous evening or the length of time since they had been gathered had withered them, and I found that they had an exquisite and very special scent. I breathed in their perfume, one by one. They were damp, so I put them to my eyes to feel the cool, for my blood was seething and my wearied limbs were as sensitive as burns to the contact of the bedclothes. Then, not knowing what to do, and not wishing to wake her, for I experienced a strange pleasure in watching her sleep, I gently placed all the violets on Marie's breast, and soon she was quite covered with them. Those lovely faded flowers she was sleeping under I saw as her symbol. Just as they gave off a particularly harsh, particularly exciting perfume despite their vanished freshness, or perhaps even because of it, so did she. The unhappiness that must have passed over her made her beautiful with the bitterness that her mouth preserved even in sleep, beautiful with the two wrinkles at the back of her neck which by day she doubtless hid beneath her hair. Contemplating this woman so sad in pleasure, whose embraces, even, were a mournful enjoyment, I divined a thousand terrible passions that must have riven her like lightning, to judge from the traces left. I thought I would enjoy hearing her tell of her life, since what I sought for in human existence was its vibrant pulsating side, the world of grand passions and beautiful tears.

At that moment, she awoke. All the violets fell from her. She smiled, her eyes still half-closed, and she put her arms around my neck and embraced me in a long morning kiss, the kiss of a waking dove.

When I begged her to tell me her story, she said:

*　　*　　*

"To you I can. Other women would lie: they would begin by telling you that they have not always been what they are; they would invent stories about their families and their loves; but I will not deceive you nor pretend that I am a princess. Listen: you shall see if I have been happy! Do you know that I have often been tempted to kill myself? Once they broke into my room and I was half asphyxiated. Oh, if I were not frightened of hell, I would have done it long ago. I am frightened of dying, too—the actual moment terrifies me, and yet I want to be dead!

"I come from the country; our father was a farmer. Before my first communion I was sent to herd the cows in the fields every morning. I was alone all day. I would sit and sleep on the bank of a ditch, or I would go bird-nesting in the woods. I climbed trees like a boy; my clothes were always in tatters. Often I was beaten for stealing apples or letting the cows into the neighbour's pastures. At harvest-time they danced round dances in the yard, and I listened to songs in which there were things I did not understand, the boys kissed the girls, there was much loud laughter. It all saddened me, brought me dreams. Sometimes as I was going home, I begged a lift in a hay-wain; the man would take me up and set me on the bundles of lucerne. Would you believe it? I began to experience an indescribable pleasure whenever I felt myself lifted from the ground by a pair of strong rough hands belonging to some sturdy lad with sunburned face and sweaty chest. Usually his sleeves would be rolled up to the armpits, and I enjoyed touching the muscles that formed humps and hollows at every movement of his hand, and being kissed by him, and feeling my cheek rasped by his beard. At the bottom of the meadow where I went every day a little brook ran between two rows of poplars, on its banks grew every sort of flower: I made bouquets, wreaths, chains of them; I used to make myself necklaces of rowanberries; it became a perfect mania, my skirt was always filled with them, and my father used to scold me and say I would never be anything but a coquette. I used to put them in my little room, too, and sometimes this abundance of scents intoxicated me and I swooned into a daze, but I enjoyed the uneasy feeling. The fragrance of mown hay, for example, of warm fermenting hay, always seemed to me so delicious that on Sundays I would shut myself up in the barn and spend my whole afternoon watching the spiders spin their webs on the beams and listening to the

hum of the flies. I lived an idle life, but I became a handsome girl, radiant with health. Often I was seized with
a kind of madness, and ran and ran till I dropped, or I
sang at the top of my lungs, or talked to myself for hours
on end. I was possessed by strange desires; I would
watch the pigeons making love on their cote, and some of
them came right up to my window, preened themselves
in the sun and sported in the vine. All night I heard the
beating of their wings and their cooing, which sounded
so sweet, so gentle, that I longed to be a pigeon like them
and turn my neck as they did to exchange kisses. 'What
do they say to each other,' I wondered, 'that they seem
so happy?' and I remembered too how proudly horses I
had seen ran after the mares, how wide their nostrils were
distended; I remembered how joyfully the wool of the
sheep would quiver as a ram came near, and the murmur
of the bees when they hung in swarms on the trees in the
orchard. I often slipped in among the animals in the
stable to breathe their vital, steamy smell, and as I fur-
tively examined their bodies my senses would grow dizzy.
At other times the very trees in the woodland glades took
on strange shapes, especially at twilight: sometimes arms
stretching to the sky, sometimes the trunk twisted like a
body beneath the wind's blasts. When I awoke at night
and there was a moon and clouds, I saw things in the sky
that terrified and allured me. I remembered that once, on
Christmas Eve, I saw a great naked woman standing
there with rolling eyes; she was quite a hundred feet tall,

but she moved, growing longer and thinner as she went, and finally dissolved, each limb remaining there apart; the head flew off first while the rest still moved. Or else I dreamed: even at ten I had feverish nights, nights of wanton dreams. Was it not wantonness that shone in my eyes, flowed in my blood, made my heart leap at the caress of one limb on another? Into my ear it sang eternal songs of delight; in my visions flesh shone like gold, unknown shapes quivered like spilt quicksilver.

"At church I gazed on the naked man spread on the cross, and I lifted his head, filled out his hips, coloured all his limbs, raised his eyelids; I created before me a splendid man with a gaze of flame; I took him down from the cross, I made him come down to me, the incense on the altar haloed him as he approached in the smoke, and sensual quivers ran over my flesh.

"When a man spoke to me, I always watched his eyes and the way they gleamed; most of all I liked those whose eyelids perpetually quivered, concealing and revealing the pupil, that movement like the beating of a moth's wings. I tried to discover the secret of their sex through their clothes, and asked my young girl friends about it; I spied on my mother's and father's kisses and the sounds from their bed at night.

"At twelve I took my first communion. A fine white dress had been brought from the city; we all wore blue sashes. I had insisted on having my hair put up in curl-papers, like a lady. Before I set out I looked at myself in

85

the glass: I was lovely as Love, I almost fell in love with myself, I wished that I could. It was about Corpus-Christi. The nuns had filled the church with flowers; the place was fragrant with them. I myself had worked with the others for three days decorating a little table with jasmin, where we were to make our vows. The altar was covered with hyacinths, the choir steps were carpeted. We all wore white gloves and each held a candle. I was very happy, I felt that this was what I was made for. Throughout Mass I kept moving my feet over the carpet, for there was none in my father's house. I would have liked to lie down on it in my beautiful dress and stay in the church alone amid the lighted candles. My heart beat with a new hope, I waited anxiously for the Host, for I had heard that first communion brought some change, and I believed that after the sacrament all my desires would be calmed. But no! When I returned to my seat, I was still burning. I had noticed the admiring glances directed at me as I went up to the priest. I feasted on them, I was aware of my beauty, priding myself confusedly on all the delights hidden within me and as yet unknown to myself.

"Coming out of Mass, we paraded in line in the grave-yard. Parents and onlookers stood in the grass on both sides to watch us go by. I walked ahead, as I was the tallest. I ate no dinner; my heart was heavy. My mother had cried during the service, and her eyes were still red. Some of the neighbours came to congratulate me and embraced me effusively; I found their caresses repugnant. That evening at Vespers there were still more people than in the morning. The boys were placed facing us and they gazed at us greedily, at me most of all: even with my eyes lowered I could feel their stare. Their hair, too, had been curled, and like us they were dressed especially for the event. When they took up their part after we had sung the first verse of a psalm, their voices lifted my soul, and when they died down, my enjoyment died with them and sprang up anew when they began again. I pronounced the vows: all that I remember is that I spoke of a white dress and innocence."

Marie stopped here, lost no doubt in the emotion of the memory, afraid of being overcome by it. Then she continued with a despairing laugh: "Ah, that white dress! It was worn out long ago! And the innocence with it! Where are the others now? Some are dead, others are married and have children; I see none of them any more, I know no one. Every New Year's Day I still want to write to my mother, but I dare not—and then—bah!— it's all stupid sentimentality!"

Mastering her emotion, she went on:
"Next day, which was also a holiday, a schoolfellow came to play with me. My mother said to me: 'Now that you are a big girl, you mustn't go about with the boys any more,' and she separated us. It took no more than

that to make me fall in love with him. I sought him out, I courted him, longed to run away with him; he was to marry me when I grew up, I called him my husband, my lover: but he was afraid. One day we were coming back alone from the woods where we had gone to pick straw-berries; as we passed a hay-rick, I flung myself on him, and, covering him with all my body, I kissed his mouth and cried: 'Love me, let's get married, let's get married!' He broke from me and ran off.

"After that I kept away from everybody and left the farm no more. I lived alone with my desires as others with their delights. When there was talk of so-and-so having carried off a girl who had been refused to him, I imagined myself his mistress; sitting behind him on his horse, I fled with him across country, I pressed him in my arms. If there was talk of a marriage, I slipped quickly into the white bed; like the bride, I trembled with fear and delight. I even envied the plaintive lowing of the cows when they calved: dreaming of the cause, I was jealous of their pangs.

"At that time my father died and my mother took me to the city with her, and my brother left to join the army, where he became a captain. I was sixteen when we left home. I bade goodbye for ever to the wood, to the meadow and my brook, goodbye to the church porch where I had spent such happy hours playing in the sun, goodbye too to my little room. I have never seen them again. The grisettes of the quarter who became my friends showed me their lovers; I went on excursions with them, I watched them making love, and I gloated on the sight. Every day I found some new pretext to be out of the house. My mother quite realized it, and at first reproached me, but finally left me in peace.

"At last one day an old woman whom I had known for some time proposed to make my fortune, saying that she had found me a wealthy lover, and that I had only to go out next evening as if I were going to deliver some work to an outlying part of the town and she would take me to him.

"I thought I should go mad in the twenty-four hours that followed. As the hour approached, the minutes lengthened; I had only one thought in my head: A lover! A lover! I was going to have a lover, I was going to be loved and that meant I was going to love! First I put on my daintiest slippers, but finding that my feet looked ungainly I changed to shoes; I arranged my hair in a hundred styles, in twists, then in bangs, in curls, in plaits.

"The more I looked at myself in the glass, the lovelier I became; but I was not lovely enough, my clothes were common, and I blushed for shame. Why was I not one of those marvellously pale women in velvet and lace, smelling of amber and rose, with rustling silks and servants in liveries of gold! I cursed my mother, my past life, and I rushed out, driven by all the temptations of the devil, savouring them all in advance.

"A carriage was awaiting us at the turn of a street. We

got in. An hour later it put us down at the grille of a park. After we had strolled for some time, I discovered that the old woman had left me, and I was walking up and down the paths alone. There were tall trees and thick foliage; strips of turf enclosed borders of flowers. I had never seen such a beautiful garden. A river flowed through it; stones, cleverly disposed here and there, formed cascades; swans were at play on the water, pluming their wings as they let the current carry them along. I enjoyed looking at the aviary, where birds of all kinds called and swung on their perches; they spread their plumed tails and paraded before each other: it was a dazzling sight. At the foot of the staircase two white marble statues faced one another in enchanting attitudes; the great pool opposite was gold in the setting sun and invited one to bathe. I thought of the unknown lover who lived there; I expected to see some beautiful man with a stride like Apollo's issue at any moment from behind a cluster of trees. After dinner, when the sounds I had been hearing in the château died down, my master appeared. He was a white-headed skinny old man, buttoned into clothes that were too tight, with the decoration of some order on his coat and trouser-straps that prevented him from bending his knees. He had a great nose and small, green, evil-looking eyes. He smiled as he accosted me: he had no teeth. When one smiles, one must have a rosy little mouth like yours, with a touch of moustache at the corners, must one not, my angel?

"We sat down on a bench together, he took my hands and found them so pretty that he kissed each finger. He told me that if I would be his mistress, be a good girl and live with him, I should be very rich, I should have servants at my command and beautiful dresses every day, horses to ride and coaches to drive out in; but for that, said he, I must love him. I promised that I would love him.

"And yet I felt none of those inner flames that had always scorched me at the approach of a man. By sitting there beside him and telling myself that I was to be his mistress, I finally achieved the desire to be so. When he suggested going in, I rose eagerly. He was delighted, he trembled with joy, the poor fellow! Passing through a fine drawing-room furnished all in gold, he led me to my room and wanted to undress me himself. He began by taking off my hat, but when he wished to undo my shoes, he could bend only with difficulty, and said to me: 'I am old, my child.' He was on his knees, his eyes besought me. He murmured, clasping his hands: 'You are so pretty!' I was afraid of what was to come.

"There was an enormous bed in the depths of the alcove. He drew me to it, uttering little cries. I felt drowned in the quilts and coverlets, his body weighed horribly on me, his flabby lips covered me with cold kisses, the ceiling of the room crushed me. How happy he was! The ecstasy he swooned in! I tried to find enjoyment myself, and in that way I apparently excited him;

but what did I care for *his* pleasure! It was mine that I wanted, mine that I expected; I sought it from his hollow mouth and his feeble limbs, I called out all that there was in this old man, but even by summoning up with incredible effort every bit of my sensuality I achieved no more than disgust on my first night of debauch.

"Hardly had he left when I got up, went to the window, opened it and cooled my skin in the air. I longed that the ocean might wash me clean of him. I remade my bed, carefully effacing all the places where that corpse had wearied me with its convulsions. I spent the whole night in tears; in my despair I roared like a castrated tiger. Ah, if you had come then! If we had known each other then! If only you had been the same age as I! We should have loved then, when I was sixteen, when my heart was new! We would have spent our whole lives at it, my arms would have been exhausted from pressing you to me, and my eyes from gazing into yours."

She went on:
"A great lady now, I rose at noon; I had a footman who followed me everywhere and a barouche with cushions to loll on; my thoroughbred was a marvellous jumper, and the black plume of my Amazon hat nodded gracefully. But since I had become wealthy overnight, all this luxury excited me instead of bringing me peace. Soon I was notorious, there were rivalries for me, my lovers performed a thousand follies to please me. Every

evening I read the love-letters of the day, hoping to find in one of them something that was different, the expression of a heart not formed like all the rest, a heart made for me. But all the men were the same. I knew beforehand how they would end their sentences and how they would fall on their knees. Two that I repulsed for a whim killed themselves: their deaths did not touch me in the slightest —why should they have died? Why didn't they go to some extreme to have me? Were I to love a man there would not be seas broad enough nor walls high enough to prevent me from reaching him. How well I should have known, had I been a man, how to corrupt guards, climb to windows by night and stifle the cries of my victim beneath my mouth—I, disabused each morning of the hopes I had had the night before!

"I drove them away angrily and took others. The sameness of pleasure drove me to despair, I pursued it frenziedly, forever thirsting after new delights magnificently dreamed of, like sailors in distress who drink sea-water and cannot keep from drinking it—so scorched are they by their thirst!

"Dandies and rustics—I wanted to see if they were all the same. I knew the passion of men with plump white hands and dyed hair plastered on their temples; I was swooned over by pale blond adolescents as effeminate as girls. Old men fouled me with their decrepit enjoyments, and I would awake to find them wheezing and rheumy-eyed beside me. Rough hands embraced me more than once on the wooden bench of a village inn, between a jug of wine and a pipe of tobacco, and for such I knew how to make myself cheap and easy; but the mob makes love no better than their masters, and a pile of hay is no warmer than a sofa. To make some of them more ardent, I devoted myself to them like a slave, but they loved me none the more for that: I degraded myself for fools, and in return they hated and despised me while I longed to multiply my favours a hundredfold and flood them with happiness. At last, in the hope that the deformed might love better than others, that the twisted might cling to life through pleasure, I gave myself to humpbacks, to dwarfs; I took blacks; to all of them I gave nights that a millionaire would envy, but perhaps I frightened them, for soon they left me. Neither the poor nor the rich, neither the handsome nor the ugly could satisfy my need for love; of them all—the weak, the languid, creatures conceived in boredom, freaks begotten by paralytics, whom wine intoxicates and woman kills, who fear that bed may be fatal to them, like a war—there was not one who was not tired after the first hour. Do the divine youths of old no longer exist on earth? No Bacchus, no Apollo, no more of those heroes who marched naked, crowned with vine and laurel? I was born to be the mistress of an emperor; I should have had the love of a bandit on a rock under an African sun; I longed for the intertwining of snakes, for the kisses exchanged by roaring lions.

"At that period, I read much. Two books especially I reread a hundred times: *Paul and Virginia* and another called *The Crimes of the Queens*. In it were depicted Messalina, Theodora, Margaret of Burgundy, Mary Stuart and Catherine II. 'To be a queen!' I cried, 'to have the mob mad for you!' Well, I have been a queen, as far as one may be a queen today; when I entered my box and granted the audience an arrogant, provocative glance, a thousand heads followed the movement of my eyebrows, and I dominated all by the insolence of my beauty.

"However, being tired of always pursuing a lover, although I desired one more than ever and at any cost, and, besides, since I had made vice a torture that was dear to me, I fled here, my heart as much aflame as if I still had a virginity to sell. Exquisite as I had become, I resigned myself to hard living; wealthy as I had been, I lay down in poverty; for by descending so low perhaps I would no longer aspire always to rise: as my body wore out, probably my desires would be calmed, and I hoped by this means to have done with them at one stroke, and to conceive an everlasting disgust for what I longed for so fervently. Yes, I who have bathed in strawberries and milk came here to lie on the common cot in the public passage. From being mistress of one man, I made myself servant to all, and how rude a master I have taken! No more fires in the winter, no more delicate wine with my meals; I wear the same dress the year through—what matter? Is it not my trade to be naked? But do you know my last thought, my last hope? Ah! I set my heart on it—it was to find one day what I had never yet met with, the man who has fled me, whom I have pursued in dandies' beds and in the balconies of theatres; the chimera that exists only in my heart and that I want to hold in my hands: one fine day, I hoped, someone would surely come —he must exist amid all those multitudes—stronger, nobler, greater than they; his eyes would be wide as a sultana's, his voice would sound a lascivious melody, his limbs would have the terrible delicious suppleness of the leopard, he would breathe perfumes to make one swoon, and his teeth would rapturously bite this breast that swells for him. As each arrived, I asked myself, 'Is it he?' And then again, 'Is it he? Let him love me! let him love me! Let him beat me, break me! I will be a whole seraglio to him in myself; I know what flowers excite, what drinks exalt, how weariness itself is transformed into delicious ecstasy; I will be a coquette when he so desires it, to excite his vanity or amuse his wit; then suddenly he will find me languorous, pliant as a reed, breathing soft words and tender sighs; for him I will twist like a serpent, at night I will have clutchings of furious delight and rending spasms. In some hot land, as we drink fine wine from crystal goblets, I will dance Spanish dances for him to the castanets, or I will leap, crying a war chant, like a savage woman; if he loves statues and pictures, I will take the poses of great masters for him to kneel before; if he prefers me to be his friend, I will dress as a man and hunt with him; I will help him in his vendettas; if he wants to kill, I will set the trap; if he is a thief, we will steal together. I will love his clothes, the cloak in which he is wrapped.' But no! never! never!

"Time rolled on and morning followed morning, and every part of my body was used in vain in the course of the pleasures on which men feast, and I remained as I was at ten, a virgin, if a virgin is one who has no husband, no lover, who has never known pleasure and dreams of it incessantly, who conjures up alluring phantoms and sees them in her reveries, who hears their voice in the noise of the winds, who seeks their lineaments in the face of the moon. I am a virgin! You laugh? But have I not virginity's dim presentiments, its ardent languors? I have everything, except virginity itself.

"See all those scratches on the mahogany at the head of my bed: they are the nail marks of all those who have struggled in it, whose heads have rubbed against it. I have never had anything in common with them. Though bound together in the closest union human arms can grant, some chasm has always divided me from them. Ah, how many times while they longed frenziedly to drown themselves utterly in their enjoyment, my mind was a thousand leagues away sharing a savage's mat or the sheepskin in some shepherd's cave in the Abruzzi.

"Not one of them, of course, comes here for *me*, not one knows *me*; perhaps they seek in me a certain woman, as I seek in them a certain man. Is there not more than one dog wandering the streets, sniffing at refuse to find a chicken bone and bits of meat? In the same way, who can tell how many exalted loves swoop down on a common harlot, how often the 'Bonjour' addressed to her marks the end of a beautiful elegy? How many I have seen come here, their hearts heavy with despair and their eyes full of tears! One, after some ball, to compress into a single woman all those he has just left; another, after seeing a wedding, exalted by the idea of innocence; and young men, too, to touch, in me, the mistresses to whom they dare not speak, shutting their eyes and seeing her in their hearts; husbands, to recover their youth and savour the easy pleasures of their prime; devil-driven priests, seeking not a woman but a courtesan, sin incarnate; they curse me, they fear me and they adore me; their temptation would be even stronger and their terror even greater if only I had a cloven foot and a gown glittering with precious stones. All these pass sadly, monotonously, like a series of shadows, like a crowd of which nothing is remembered except the sound it made, the shuffling of its thousands of feet, its confused clamour. Do I know the name of even one of them? They come and they go; never is there a disinterested caress, and of course they demand caresses—they would demand love if they dared! One has to tell them they are handsome, pretend to assume they are rich, and they smile. They like to laugh, too: sometimes I have to sing, or be silent, or speak. No one has ever suspected that there might be a heart in a woman so notorious. Imbeciles!—who praised the arc of my eyebrow and the splendour of my shoulder, delighted to have a king's dish so cheap, and yet failed to take the inextinguishable love that was there before them, flung at their very feet!

"Yet I see some women even here who have lovers, real lovers who love them; they keep a separate place for them in their bed as in their hearts, and when they come to them they are happy. It is for them, you see, that they spend so long combing their hair and watering the flower pots at their windows; but I have no one, no one! Not even the tranquil affection of some poor child, for I am pointed out to them as the prostitute, and they pass me with averted head. How long it is since I have walked through the fields and seen the country! How many Sundays I have spent listening to the sad sound of the bells calling to the services I attend no more! How long it is since I have heard the cowbells in the copses. Ah! I want to go far, far away from here; I am so sick of it all, so sick of it! I will go on foot, I will go back to my nurse; she is a good woman; she will welcome me. When I was small I used to go to her and she gave me milk; I will help her bring up children and keep her house, I will gather dead wood in the forest, we will warm our-selves at the fireside on snowy nights; winter will soon be here, on Twelfth Night we will cut our cake. Oh! she will love me well, I will rock the little ones to sleep for her—how happy I shall be!"

She was silent; then lifted to me a gaze sparkling through her tears, as if to say: "Is it you?"

I had listened greedily, I had watched the words issue from her mouth, trying to identify myself with the life they described. Suddenly magnified to the proportions I myself had doubtless given her for the moment, she seemed a new woman, full of unknown mysteries; and, despite my relations with her, one endowed with all the fascination of an exciting magic and a new allurement. Indeed the men who had possessed her had left upon her, as it were, the scent of a dying perfume, traces of vanished passions, that gave her a voluptuous majesty: debauch adorned her with an infernal beauty. Without those past orgies would she have had that suicide's smile that made one think of a dead woman awakening to love? Her cheek was the paler for them, her hair the softer and the more fragrant, her limbs the suppler, smoother, warmer. Like me, she had gone from joy to desperation, from hope to disgust; nameless despair had succeeded mad ecstasy. Unknown to one another, she in her prostitution, I in my chastity, we had followed the same road that ended in the same abyss: while I had been seeking a mistress, she had been seeking a lover, she in the world, I in my heart, and both had eluded us.

"Poor woman," I said, pressing her to me, "how you must have suffered!"

"Have you suffered so?" she asked. "Are you as I am? Have you, too, often soaked your pillow with tears? Are sunny winter days so sad for you too? When I walk alone on foggy evenings, I sometimes think the rain is piercing my very heart and making it fall in fragments.

"I doubt, though, that the world has ever been so stale for you as it has for me. You have had your days of pleasure, but for me it has been as if I had been born in prison; I have a thousand things in me that have never seen the light.

"But you are so young! All the men are old nowadays, children are as disillusioned as old men, our mothers were bored when they conceived us. People were not like that in the old days, were they?"

"That is true," I replied. "The houses we live in are all alike, white and mournful as tombs in a churchyard. In the dark old hovels they are tearing down life must have been warmer: they sang loud, smashed jugs on the tables, broke the beds with their love-making?"

"But who is making you so sad? You have been much in love?"

"In love, my God! Enough to envy you your life."

"Envy my life!" she said.

"Yes, envy it! For perhaps I should have been happy in your place; for if a man such as you desire does not exist, a woman such as I wish for must live somewhere;

among so many beating hearts, there must be one to beat for me."

"Seek it! Seek it!"

"Oh, yes, I have loved! So much that I am saturated with repressed desires. No, you will never know how many women have driven me to distraction, women whom I cherished in the depths of my heart with an angelic love. When I spent a day with a woman, I would say to myself: 'Why did I not know her ten years ago! All those earlier days of hers belonged to me, her first smile should have been for me, her first thought in the world for me. People come and talk with her, she answers them, she thinks of them. I should have read the books she admires. Why have I not walked with her in all the shady groves that have sheltered her? There are dresses she has worn out, and I have not seen them; she has heard the most beautiful operas, and I was not there; others have already given her flowers to smell that I did not gather; I shall be able to do nothing, she will forget me, to her I am as a passer-by in the street. And when I was not with her, I said to myself: 'Where is she? What is she doing all day, far from me? How is she spending her time?' Let a woman love a man, let her but make him a sign, and he will fall at her feet! But what a rare chance it is for us if she looks at us! . . . For that, a man must be rich, keep horses, have a house adorned with statues, give parties, fling away gold, make a sensation; but to live amid the crowd without being able to dominate it by genius or by money, and to remain as unknown as the most cowardly and the most imbecile, when one aspires to divine love, when one would die joyfully under the eyes of a loved woman—that is the torture I have known."

"You are shy, aren't you? They frighten you."

"No longer. Once the very sound of their footsteps made me tremble. I would stand in front of a hairdresser's gazing at the beautiful wax figures with flowers and diamonds in their hair, pink, white, their gowns cut low: I have been in love with some of them. A shoemaker's window would send me into ecstasies, too: in the little satin slippers to be carried off for a ball that evening I would imagine a naked foot, a ravishing foot with delicate nails, a foot of living alabaster, that of a princess entering her bath. And corsets swaying in the wind outside dress shops filled me with strange desire. I have offered bouquets of flowers to women I did not love, hoping that love would come that way, as I had heard it might. I have written letters addressed to any woman at random, to summon up my tears by writing—and they came. The least smile of a woman's lips made my heart melt deliciously—and then, that was all! So much happiness was not for me. Who could love me?"

"Wait! Wait a year yet, six months! Tomorrow perhaps! Hope on!"

"I have hoped too much to attain my hopes."

"You talk like a child," she said.

"No, I cannot picture any love that wouldn't weary me after twenty-four hours. I have longed so much for love that I am tired of it, as one tires of those whom one has cherished too deeply."

"And yet love is the only truly good thing in the world."

"No one knows that better than I. I would give anything to spend a single night with a woman who would love me."

"Oh, if you would let all the generosity and goodness in your heart be seen, instead of hiding it, every woman would want you, there is not one who would not try to be your mistress. But you have been even more foolish than I! Does anyone take notice of buried treasures? Only coquettes discover the secret of men like you, and they torture them; the others do not see it. And yet you well deserve to be loved! Now . . . Yes! I will love you! I will be your mistress!"

"My mistress?"

"I beseech you! I will follow you where you will, I will leave this place, rent a room opposite yours, watch you all day. How I will love you! To be with you in the evening, in the morning; at night to sleep together in each other's arms; to eat at the same table, facing one another; to dress in the same room, to go out together, to feel you beside me! Are we not made for each other? Do not your hopes match my disillusions? Is not your life like mine? You will tell me all your torments of loneliness, I will tell over the sufferings I have endured; we must live as if we had only one hour to be together, exhaust all the tenderness and all the passion there is in us, and then begin over again and die together. Kiss me, kiss me again! Lay your head on my heart, let me feel its weight there; I want to feel your hair caressing my neck, I want to glide my hands over your shoulders: your eyes are so tender!"

The crumpled bed-cover hung to the floor, leaving our feet bare. She rose on her knees and tucked it under the mattress, and I saw her white back bend like a reed. The sleepless night had exhausted me; my head ached; my eyes were burning, and she kissed them gently with the tips of her lips, cooling them as if they had been moistened with cold water. She, too, was waking more and more from the torpor to which she had briefly abandoned herself. Excited by weariness, inflamed by the taste of the caresses that had gone before, she strained me to her with desperate sensuality, saying, "Let us love each other since no one has loved us! You are mine!" Panting, her mouth open, she kissed me furiously; then, suddenly regaining possession of herself, she passed her hand over her scattered tresses, and added:

"Listen. How lovely our life would be if we were to go and live in a land where yellow flowers bloom in the sun and oranges ripen on a shore—it seems there are such places—a shore where the sand is dazzling white, the men wear turbans, the women gauzy dresses. We would lie beneath some great broad-leaved tree, we would listen to the sound of the sea, walk together beside the waves and gather seashells, I would make baskets of reeds that you would sell. I would dress you, curl your hair with my fingers, put a necklace round your neck—Oh, how I would love you! How I love you! Let me take my fill of you!"

Pressing me violently to the bed, she fell upon my entire body, stretching herself against it with obscene enjoyment, and, pale, shivering, with clenched teeth, she clasped me to her with frantic strength. I felt myself swept away in a hurricane of love, there were shattering sobs, then piercing cries. My lips were moist and bright and voracious; our muscles were knotted together; we became one; pleasure turned to delirium, enjoyment to torture.

Suddenly she opened wondering, terrified eyes, and said: "What if I should have a child!"

And then changing, passing to coaxing supplication: "Yes, yes, a child! A child of yours! . . . You are leaving me? We shall never see each other again, you will never come back—will you think of me sometimes? I shall always have the lock of your hair. Goodbye! Wait, it is hardly day."

Why was I so eager to flee? Did I love her already? Marie spoke not another word, though I stayed with her for quite half an hour more. Perhaps she was thinking of the absent lover. There comes a moment before parting when by the anticipation of sadness one's beloved is already gone.

We did not say goodbye. I took her hand. She responded, but the strength to press mine was locked in her heart.

I never saw her again.

*　　*　　*

I have thought of her since: not a day has passed without my spending as many hours as possible dreaming of her. Sometimes I shut myself up alone especially for it, and try to live again in the memory; often I force myself to think of her before I fall asleep, hoping to dream of her at night, but that happiness I have never attained.

I have sought her everywhere, among the parading strollers, at the theatre, at street corners; without knowing why, I thought she would write to me; when I heard a carriage stop at my door, I imagined that it would be she who stepped out. With what emotion I followed certain women! With what racing of my heart I turned my head to see if it were she!

The house was torn down, and no one could tell me what had become of her.

The desire for a woman one has possessed is a frightful thing, a thousand times worse than the other: terrible images haunt you like pangs of remorse. I am not jealous of the men who had her before me, but I am jealous of those who have had her since; a tacit agreement, it seems to me, bound us to be faithful to each other; I kept this pact for more than a year, and then chance, boredom, perhaps the lassitude of that very emotion, made me break it. But it was she that I pursued everywhere: in the beds of others I dreamed of her caresses.

In vain one sows new passions over old. These will always reappear, there is no power in the world that can tear up their roots. The Roman roads the consular chariots rolled on have long been in disuse, a thousand new paths cross them, fields have risen over them, corn grows on them, but their traces are still visible, and their great stones shatter the ploughshares at tilling time.

The type of woman that almost all men seek is perhaps merely the memory of a love conceived in heaven or in the first days of life. The second woman to please you almost always resembles the first, and one needs a great degree of corruption or a very vast heart to love everything. See too how writers speak eternally of the same women and describe them a hundred times without ever tiring of them. I knew a friend who had, at fifteen, adored a young mother he had seen nursing her child; for many years he valued none but plump figures, the beauty of slim women was odious to him.

As time went on, I loved her more and more. With the mania one has for impossibilities, I made up adventures to find her again; I imagined our meeting. I saw her eyes again in the blue bubbles of the river, and the tints of her face in the aspen leaves coloured by autumn. Once as I was walking quickly through a meadow and the grass swished about my feet she was behind me; I turned round—there was no one there. Another day a carriage passed before my eyes. I raised my head, a great white veil blew through the window and waved in the wind; the wheels turned, the veil swirled, it called to me, it disappeared—and I fell back, alone, despairing, more solitary than if I had been at the bottom of some abyss.

Ah, if one could draw out from oneself all that one has within one and create a being of thought alone! If one could hold one's phantom in one's hands, touch its brow, instead of wasting on air so many caresses, so many sighs! Far from it: memory forgets, the image fades, but the agony of sorrow lives on. It is to recall her that I have written this, hoping that words would make her live again for me. I have failed. I know far more than I have told.

It is a thing that I have never confided to anyone, for they would have laughed at me. Are they not mocked, who love? For men are somehow ashamed of loving: through shyness or through selfishness each conceals the best and most delicate notions of his soul; to gain esteem, one must show only the ugliest aspects, for that is the means by which one attains the common level. "Love a woman of that kind?" they would have said; and of course no one would have understood. So what is the good of speaking about it?

They would have been right. She was perhaps neither more beautiful nor more ardent than any other. I am afraid now lest I am in love only with a concept of my imagination, cherishing in her nothing but the love she made me dream of.

I long struggled under the thought, I had placed love too high to hope that it might come down to me; but, from the persistence of this idea, I have had to recognize that something of this sort must be so. It was not until some months after I left her that I felt it; during the first days, indeed, I lived in complete tranquillity.

How empty the world is for him who walks alone! What was I to do? How was I to pass my time? On what was I to busy my brain? How long the days are! Where is the man who complains of the shortness of the days of life? Show him to me, for he must be a happy mortal.

Find some distraction, they say: but in what? It is like saying to me, try to be happy: but how? What is the good of all this activity? All is well in Nature: the trees grow, the rivers flow, the birds sing, the stars shine; but tormented man is ever in motion, lays low the forests, upturns the earth, flings himself upon the sea, travels, runs to and fro, kills animals, kills himself, and he weeps, he howls, he thinks of hell, as if God had given him an imagination to conceive even more evils than he already endures!

In the beginning, before Marie, my melancholy had some fine, some grand quality: now it is stupid, the melancholy of a man soaked in cheap brandy, the sleep of a dead drunk.

Those who have lived much are not like me. At fifty they are fresher than I am at twenty; for them all is still new and alluring.

Am I like those worthless horses that are tired when they have hardly left the stable, and trot easily only after they have covered some distance limping and suffering? Too many sights make me suffer and too many inspire me with pity—or rather, they are all mingled for me in a common disgust.

He who is sufficiently well born not to want a mistress because he cannot cover her with diamonds nor lodge her in a palace, who watches the loves of the vulgar and contemplates with a tranquil eye the bestial ugliness of those two rutting animals that are called a lover and a mistress, is not tempted to demean himself so low. He avoids love as a weakness and tramples underfoot all the desires which assail him; and this struggle exhausts him. The cynical egoism of men keeps me apart from them, just as the limited mentality of women disgusts me with their conversation; yet, after all, I am wrong, for a pair of lovely lips is worth more than all the eloquence in the world.

III

The falling leaf flutters and flies off in the wind, just as I would like to fly off, go, go and never return, go it matters not where; but I would leave my country; my home weighs on shoulders, I have gone in and out of the same door so many times! I have raised my eyes so many times to the same spot in the ceiling of my room that it must be quite worn away.

Oh, to feel yourself swaying on the camel's back! Before you a deep red sky and deep brown sand, the flaming horizon stretching ahead, the country undulating, the eagle swooping over your head; in one quarter of the sky a flock of rosy-legged storks passing on their way to the wells. The swaying of the ship of the desert lulls you, the sun makes you close your eyes, bathes you in its rays. All you hear is the muffled tread of the animals. The leader has just ended his song: we ride and ride, on and on. At evening stakes are planted, tents pitched, the dromedaries are watered; we stretch out on a lion skin, we smoke, we light fires to keep off the jackals we hear howling in the depths of the desert. Unknown stars, four times as big as ours, throb in the skies. In the morning the water-skins are refilled at the oasis; we set off again; we are alone; the wind whistles and the sand rises in whorls.

And then, in some plain over which we have galloped all day, palms rise between pillars; their branches wave softly beside the motionless shade of ruined temples. Goats climb on the fallen pediments and munch the weeds that have grown up in the marble carvings; they leap off in flight when you approach. Then, after passing through forests of trees linked by gigantic lianas, after crossing rivers so broad their further bank is not to be seen, you come to the Sudan, the land of Negroes, the land of gold. But on! I long to see furious Malabar and its dances of death: the wines are as deadly as poison, the poisons are sweet as wine; the sea, a blue sea full of pearls and coral, re-echoes the clamour of the sacred orgies celebrated in the mountain-caves. There is not a wave stirring, the air is vermilion, the cloudless sky is mirrored in the warm ocean; cables steam when they are drawn up out of the water, sharks follow the ship and batten on the dead.

Oh India! India above all! White mountains, pagodas and idols in the midst of jungles full of tigers and elephants, yellow men in white robes, bronze-coloured women with bangles on ankle and arm, gauzy dresses that shroud them like a mist, eyes whose lids alone are visible, henna-darkened. They are singing together a chant to some god, they are dancing. . . . Dance, dance, bayadere, daughter of Ganges, let your feet turn and turn in my head! Serpent-like she coils; her arms weave, her head sways, her hips swing, her nostrils swell, her hair unrolls and falls; smoking incense veils the staring gilded idol with four heads and twenty arms.

In a cedar-wood canoe, a long canoe with paddles so slim that they seem like feathers, beneath a sail of plaited bamboos, to the sound of tom-toms and tambourines, I will go to that yellow land they call China. You can hold the women's feet in one hand, they have tiny heads, thin eyebrows that curve up at the corners; they live in arbours of green reeds and eat velvet-skinned fruits from painted porcelain. The mandarin, pointed moustache falling to his chest, head shaven, pigtail dropping low on his back, round fan between his fingers, walks slowly over rice mats in the gallery where tripods smoke; he has a little pipe in his pointed cap and black writings are printed on his red silk robes. Ah, how tea-chests have sent me travelling!

Whirl me away, oh storms of the New World, that uproot century-old oaks and set the snake-filled lakes in turmoil! May the torrents of Norway cover me with their foam! May the heavy snows of Siberia obliterate my path! Oh, to travel! to travel! to travel and never stop; to see everything loom up and disappear in this great waltz until your skin bursts and the blood flows forth!

Let valleys follow after mountains, fields after towns, plains after seas. Let us climb and descend, let cathedral spires vanish, and the masts of ships in the harbours. Let us listen to the waterfall tumbling on the rock, the wind in the forest, the glacier melting in the sun. Let me see the gallop of Arab horsemen, women borne in palanquins; swelling domes, pyramids rising to the sky, choked vaults where mummies sleep, narrow passes where the brigand loads his gun, rushes where the rattlesnake hides, the striped zebra running in the tall grass, the kangaroo on his hind legs, the monkey swinging on the end of the coconut branch, the tiger leaping on his prey, the gazelle in flight. . . .

On! On over vast oceans, where whale makes war on cachalot! Here is the savages' canoe, sweeping over the tops of the waves like a great sea bird beating its wings; bleeding scalps hang at its prow; they have painted their ribs red; their lips slashed, their faces daubed, rings in their noses, they sing, shouting the death song; their great bows are bent, their green-tipped arrows are poisoned and carry agonizing death. Their naked women, breasts and hands tattooed, raise great pyres for their husbands' victims, for they have been promised the flesh of whites, delicate to the tooth.

Where shall I go? The earth is large: I will exhaust every road, empty every horizon. Would that I might perish doubling the Cape, die of cholera at Calcutta or of the plague in Constantinople!

If only I were a muleteer in Andalusia! To amble all day among the gorges of the sierras; see the flowing Guadalquivir with its islands of oleanders; at evening listen to the guitars and the voices singing beneath the balconies; watch the moon's reflection in the marble fountains of the Alhambra, where sultanas once bathed.

Why am I not a gondolier in Venice, or driver of one of those diligences which carry you in the fine season from Nice to Rome! There are people who live in Rome, people who actually live there always. Happy the Neapolitan beggar who sleeps on the shore in the sun, and, smoking his cigars, sees the smoke of Vesuvius too rising on the sky! I envy him his bed of shingle and the dreams he may have on it; the sea, forever lovely, carries him the fragrance of its waves and the distant murmur of Capri.

Sometimes I imagine myself arriving in Sicily, in a little fishing village where all the boats have lateen sails. It is morning; a daughter of the people sits there among baskets and spread nets; she is barefoot, her bodice is laced with gold string, like the women of the Greek colonies; her black hair, divided into two tresses, falls to her heels. She rises, shakes her apron. She walks, and her figure is at once sturdy and supple, like that of a nymph of antiquity. If only I were loved by such a woman! A poor ignorant child who cannot even read, but her voice would be so sweet when she said to me, in her Sicilian accent: "I love you! Stay!"

*   *   *

The manuscript stops here, but I knew the author, and if anyone, having got through all the metaphors, hyperboles and other figures of speech, has reached this page and wishes to discover some end to it, let him read on: we will provide one.

It must be that the emotions have few words to serve

them, otherwise the book would have been finished in the first person. No doubt our young man found nothing more to say. There is a point beyond which one does not write, a point whence one proceeds only in thought; and it is at this point that he stopped—so much the worse for the reader.

I wonder at the chance that willed it that the book should have ended at the moment when it would have become better. The author was about to enter the world; he would have had a thousand things to teach us; but on the contrary he gave himself up more and more to an austere and sterile solitude. He thought fit to complain no longer—a proof, perhaps, that he was really beginning to suffer. I have found nothing either in his conversation or in his letters or in the papers I examined after his death, among which was this manuscript, nothing which might reveal his spiritual state after the time when he stopped writing his confessions.

His great regret was that he was not a painter: he asserted that he had very fine pictures in his imagination. He was in despair too at not being a musician: innumerable symphonies filled his head on spring mornings as he walked down avenues of poplars. As a matter of fact, he understood absolutely nothing of either painting or music; I have seen him admire absolute daubs and leave the Opera with a headache. With a little more time, patience, work and, above all, with a more delicate taste for the plastic in art, he might have achieved the writing of mediocre verses good enough to inscribe in a lady's album—which is always a polite accomplishment, whatever one may say about it.

In his earliest youth he had fed upon extremely bad authors, as will have been seen from his style; as he grew older, he lost the taste for them, but good writers no longer filled him with the same enthusiasm.

Passionately attached to the beautiful, he was repelled by ugliness as by a crime. Indeed, an ugly being is an atrocity, an object of horror at a distance, of disgust at close quarters: when he speaks, you suffer; if he weeps, his tears irritate you; you want to hit him when he laughs, and, silent, his motionless face seems the seat of every vice, every baser instinct. Nor did he ever forgive a man who had displeased him on first meeting: on the other hand, he was utterly devoted to people who had scarcely addressed him a word, whose way of walking or the shape of whose head he admired.

He shunned assemblies, theatres, balls, concerts; for hardly had he entered when he felt frozen with melancholy, cold to the roots of his hair. When the crowd elbowed him, a puerile hatred rose in his heart: towards this crowd his heart was that of a wolf, of a wild beast tracked to its lair.

He had the vanity to believe that men did not love him—men did not know him.

Public misfortunes and collective disasters saddened him only moderately; I would even say that he felt more pity for caged canaries beating their wings when the sun shone than for peoples in slavery: that was his nature. He was full of delicate scruples and real sensibility; for example, he could not sit in a pastry shop and see a poor fellow watch him eat without blushing to the ears; as he left he would give him all the money he had in his pocket and flee as fast as he could. But he was considered cynical because he called things by their names and said aloud what people hardly dare think.

The love of women kept by other men (the ideal of young men who have not the means to keep one themselves) was odious to him, disgusted him; he thought that the man who pays is the master, the lord, the king. Although he was poor, he respected wealth, not the wealthy. To be for nothing the lover of a woman whom another houses, dresses and feeds, seemed to him as amusing as to steal a bottle of wine from someone else's cellar. He would say that to boast of it was the mark of knavish menials and low persons.

To desire a married woman, and to that end make oneself her husband's friend, affectionately shake his hand, laugh at his puns, sympathize over his misfortunes, run errands for him, read the same paper as he, in a word, to perform in one day more mean and stupid actions than ten galley-slaves have undergone in the whole of their lives, was something too humiliating to his pride; and yet he loved several married women. Sometimes he really set out for conquest, but he would suddenly be seized by repugnance just when the lovely lady was beginning to bend a favourable eye on his suit—like May frosts that blast apricots in flower.

Well, then, the grisettes, you say? No! He could not bring himself to climb up to an attic to kiss a mouth that had just lunched on cheese, to press a chilblained hand.

As for seducing a young girl, he would have thought himself less culpable if he had raped her: to attach someone to himself was for him worse than murder. He seriously thought it was less wrong to kill a man than to beget a child: from the former you take his life, not the whole of it, but the half or the quarter or the hundredth part of an existence which is to end anyway, which would end without your intervention; but with the latter, he would say, are you not responsible for all the tears it will shed from its cradle to the grave? But for you it would not have been born, and it is born, and why? For your amusement, not for its own, certainly. To bear your name, the name of a blackguard, I wager? Better write it on a wall: three or four letters don't need a man to carry them.

In his eyes the man who, backed by the Civil Code, forces his way into the bed of the virgin handed over to him that morning, thus performing a legalized rape protected by authority, had no analogy among the monkeys, the hippopotamuses, the toads, who, male and female, couple when mutual desire drives them to seek each other and unite, where there is neither terror and disgust on the one side nor brutality and obscene despotism on the other. He set out long immoral theories on the subject which it is unnecessary to repeat here.

That is why he did not marry and took as mistress neither a kept harlot nor a married woman, neither a grizette nor a girl of good family: the thought of a widow didn't occur to him.

When he had to choose a career, he hesitated between a thousand repugnances. He was not mischievous enough to become a philanthropist, and his natural goodness of character kept him from medicine; as for commerce, he was incapable of calculation, the very sight of a bank set his nerves on edge. In spite of his follies, he had too much sense to take seriously the noble profession of attorney; besides, his justice did not correspond to that of the laws. He had too much taste to venture into criticism; he was too much of a poet, perhaps, to succeed in literature. And, after all, are these "careers"? "One must establish oneself, have some position in the world, one is bored if one remains idle, one must make oneself useful, man is born to work": maxims difficult of comprehension which people took the trouble to repeat to him over and over again.

Resigned to boredom everywhere and in everything, he declared that he wanted to study law, and went to live in Paris. Many people in his village envied him and told him that he was going to be happy frequenting the cafés, the theatres, the restaurants, seeing beautiful women. He let them talk on, smiling as one does when one would like to weep. Yet, how often had he longed to leave his room forever, the room in which he had so often yawned and rubbed his elbows on the old mahogany desk where he had composed his dramas at the age of fifteen! And he parted from it all with pain; perhaps it is the places one has most cursed that one prefers to all others: do not prisoners miss their prison? For in that prison they had hoped; now that they have left it, they hope no more. Through the walls of their cell they saw the countryside decked in daisies, threaded with streams, carpeted with yellow corn, roads bordered with trees; now, returning to freedom, to poverty, they see life as it is, miserable, harsh, dirty, cold; the countryside, too, the lovely countryside, they see as it is: decked with rural police to prevent them from plucking fruit if they are thirsty, adorned with gamekeepers in case they should wish to kill game when they are hungry, carpeted with gendarmes lest they try to take a stroll without a passport.

He went to live in a furnished room, in which the furniture had been bought for others and worn out by others: he felt as though he were living amid ruins. He spent the day working, listening to the dull rumble of the street, watching the rain falling on the roofs.

When it was sunny, he went for a stroll in the Luxembourg; he walked on the dead leaves, remembering that he had done the same at school; he had not imagined that ten years later his life would be like this. Or else he sat on a bench and dreamed of a thousand tender, melancholy things, watched the cold black water in the fountains, and returned home with a heavy heart. Two or three times, having nothing particular to do, he went into the churches at Benediction, and tried to pray; how his friends would have laughed, had they seen him dip his fingers in the stoup and make the sign of the cross!

One evening as he was wandering about a suburb, and, irritated for no reason, was wishing that he might leap on naked swords and fight to the death, he heard voices raised in song and the mellow tone of an organ blasting its reply. He went in. An old woman sitting on the ground under the porch begged for charity by rattling halfpence in a tin mug. The padded door swung to and fro as people came and went; there was a clatter of wooden shoes, a scraping of chairs on the stone floor. Beyond, the choir was illuminated, the tabernacle gleamed in the candle-light, the priest was chanting prayers, the lamps hanging in the nave swayed on their long cords. The tops of the central arches and the entire side aisles were in shadow; rain lashed the windows, rattling on the leaded panes.

The organ pealed and the voices took up their part, like that day on the cliffs when he had heard the sea and the birds speaking together. He was seized by a longing to be a priest, to preach funeral orations over the dead, to wear a hair-shirt and prostrate himself, overcome by the love of God. . . . Suddenly he felt a sneer of pity in his heart, he pulled his hat down over his ears, and went out shrugging of his shoulders.

Sadder than ever he became, longer than ever were the days. The hurdy-gurdies playing under his window tore at his very soul; he found an invincible melancholy in them, and used to say that they were filled with tears. Or rather he said nothing, for he did not act the blasé, the bored, the man who is disillusioned in everything; towards the end, indeed, people even thought that his character had become gayer. It was most often some poor fellow from a southern land, a Piedmontese, a Genoese, who turned the handle. Why had he left his aerie, his hut crowned with maize at harvest-time? He gazed at him as he played, his great square head, his black beard, his brown hands; a little monkey dressed in red leaped and grimaced on his shoulder; when the man held out his cap, he flung his alms into it and followed him until he lost sight of him.

A house was building opposite. That lasted three months. He saw the walls rise, the storeys mount one on another: panes were put in the windows, it was plastered, then painted; then the doors were shut. Families came and began to live in it, and he was annoyed at having neighbours—he preferred the sight of the stones.

He visited the museums; he contemplated all those factitious, motionless, eternally-young figures in their ideal life; the crowd comes to see them, and they watch the crowd without a movement of their heads, without raising their hand from their sword, and their eyes will still be shining when our grandchildren are buried. He would lose himself in meditation before antique statues, especially if they were mutilated.

A lamentable incident occurred. One day he thought he recognized someone walking in the street. The stranger looked likewise at him; they stopped and accosted one another. It was he! His old friend, his best friend, his brother, beside whom he had lived at school, in the classroom, the study, the dormitory. They had done their impositions and exercises together; they had walked arm in arm in the playground and out strolling: long ago they had sworn to live in common and be friends until death. First they exchanged handclasps, crying each other's name; then they scrutinized each other from head to foot in silence. Both had changed and had already aged a little.

After asking one another what they were doing, they stopped short and could go no further. They had not seen each other for six years and could not find ten words to exchange. Bored, finally, with staring at the whites of one another's eyes, they parted.

Since he had no energy for anything, and since, whatever the philosophers have said about time, he was sure that of all the world's commodities it was the least borrowable, he set to drinking brandy and smoking opium. He often spent his days prostrate, half drunk, in a state that was between apathy and nightmare.

Occasionally, strength returned to him and he would suddenly snap up like a spring. Then work seemed most attractive, and the radiance of thought made him smile the profound and placid smile of the sage. He speedily set to work; he had superb plans, he wanted to present certain periods in an entirely new light, unite art with history, criticize the great poets as well as the great painters, and to that end learn languages, descend into antiquity, penetrate the East. He saw himself already reading inscriptions and deciphering obelisks. Then he called himself a fool and folded his arms once more.

He did not read any longer, or else only books which he considered bad, yet they brought him a kind of pleasure by their very mediocrity. At night he did not sleep, but tossed on his bed with insomnia, dreamed and woke again, so that in the morning he was more tired than had he not gone to bed at all.

Worn down by boredom, that terrible habit, finding even a sort of pleasure in the apathy which is its result, he was like a man watching himself die. He no longer opened his window to breathe the air, no longer washed his hands; he lived in poverty-stricken squalor, wore the same shirt for a week, no longer shaved or combed his hair. Though liable to chills, if he went out in the morning and returned with wet feet he did not change his shoes all day or make a fire. He would fling himself fully clothed on his bed and try to sleep, watching the flies on the ceiling, smoking, and letting his eye follow the little blue spirals that issued from his lips.

It will be plainly conceived that he had no object in life: that was the trouble. What could have animated him, brought him to life? Love? He shunned it. Ambition? He laughed at it. As for money, he was really quite covetous, but his laziness carried the day, and of course a million was not worth the trouble of acquiring. Luxury suits the man born to opulence; he who has earned his fortune rarely knows how to spend it. His pride was such that he would not have wished a throne. You will ask: What did he want? I do not know, but certainly he was not thinking of getting himself elected Deputy; he would even have refused the position of Prefect, with the laced coat, the cross of honour about his neck, the ceremonial buckskin breeches and riding boots thrown in. He would rather have read André Chénier than have been a minister; he would have preferred to be Talma rather than Napoleon.

He was a man prone to fallacy and rigmarole, and he greatly misused epithets.

From certain heights, earth and all its struggles disappear. Similarly, looking down from certain sorrows, you are as nothing and you despise everything; when they do not kill you, suicide alone can deliver you from them. He did not kill himself, he went on living.

Carnival time came: but he found no diversion in it. He did everything by contradictions. Funerals almost made him laugh, while theatres filled him with gloom:

he always imagined a crowd of skeletons dressed up in gloves, cuffs and feathered hats, leaning over the rims of the boxes, quizzing one another, simpering, staring with empty eyes; in the parterre he saw a crowd of closely-packed white skulls gleaming beneath the light of the chandelier. He heard people running down the staircase, laughing as they went off with their women.

A memory of his youth returned to him: he thought of X. . . . , the village he had walked to one day, as he has related in his narrative. He wanted to revisit it before he died; for he felt he was nearing his end. He put money in his pocket, took his cloak, and set out at once. Lent had begun early that year, in February. It was still very cold and the roads were frozen. The carriage drove at a gallop. He sat in the coupé; he did not sleep, but enjoyed the sensation of being borne along and the thought of seeing the sea again. In the light of the carriage lantern he saw the postillion's reins bobbing in the air and flicking the steaming cruppers of the horses. The sky was serene, and the stars shone as though it were the most beautiful of summer nights.

About ten o'clock in the morning, he got down at Y. . . . and thence made his way on foot to X. . . . He walked quickly, this time, he even ran, to keep warm. The ditches were full of ice, the tips of the branches on the bare trees were red, and the fallen leaves rotted by the rains were a great carpet of black and steel-grey covering the floor of the forest. The sky was white and sunless. He noticed that the road-signs had been overturned; at one spot a wood-lot had been cut since he had last passed by. He quickened his pace, he was eager to arrive. At last the ground began to fall away. He took a path he knew across the fields, and soon in the distance he saw the sea. He stopped. He heard it thudding on the shore and booming far out on the horizon, *in altum*; a salty smell reached him, carried on the cold winter breeze. His heart leaped.

A new house had been built at the entry to the village, two or three others had been pulled down.

The boats were at sea, the quay was deserted, for everyone was indoors. Long icicles, which children call "kings' candles", hung from the eaves and the ends of the gutters. The signs of grocer and innkeeper creaked testily on their iron brackets; the tide was rising, and surged up on the shingle with a noise that sounded like the clanking of chains and like sobs.

After he had breakfasted—and he was surprised that he was not hungry—he went for a walk on the beach. The wind sang, the sparse rushes growing on the dunes whistled and swayed furiously. Spume flew from the breakers and scurried over the sands, and sometimes a gust blew it up towards the clouds.

Night came, or, rather, the long twilight that precedes it in the saddest days of the year. Great flakes of snow fell; they melted on the waves but stayed long on the beach, spotting it with great silver tears.

At one place he saw an old boat, half buried in the sand, which had been stranded there was twenty years perhaps; samphire had grown in it, and starfish and mussels clung to the greened timbers. He loved this boat; he walked round and round it, touched it here and there, contemplated it curiously as one contemplates a corpse.

A hundred paces away there was a little cove in a cleft in the rock where he had often sat and passed good hours doing nothing at all—he would bring a book but not read it, just lying there alone, stretched on his back, watching the blue of the sky between the sheer white walls of the rocks. There he had dreamed his sweetest dreams and listened to the cry of the gulls; there the sea grasses had shaken down on him the pearls in their hair; from there he had watched the sails sink below the horizon, and there the sun had been warmer, for him, than anywhere else on earth.

He sought out the place and found it, but others had taken possession of it: idly kicking over the sand, he uncovered a broken bottle and a knife. People had picnicked there, no doubt, had brought their girls, had lunched, laughed, joked. "Oh, God," he cried, "is there no spot on earth that we have loved enough, lived in enough, for it to belong to us until death, looked on by no eyes but ours?"

So once again he climbed the ravine where stones had often rolled down under his feet, where he had sometimes hurled them down to hear them clatter against the rocky wall and hear the lonely echo answer. On the plateau above the cliff the air was keener; he saw the moon rising opposite him in a patch of dark blue sky; below the moon, to the left, was a little star.

He wept—was it for cold or for sadness? His heart was bursting, he had to talk to someone. He went into a café where he had sometimes gone to drink beer, asked for a cigar, and could not help saying to the good woman who served him: "I have been here before." "Ah," she replied, "but this isn't the good season, sir, this isn't the good season," and she gave him his change.

In the evening he went out once more. He lay down in a hole that was used by hunters for shooting wild duck. For a moment he saw the image of the moon tossing on the waves and coiling in the sea like a great serpent: then clouds converged again from every quarter of the sky, and all was black. In the darkness, dark waves swelled, piled on each other and exploded with the roar of a hundred cannon. A kind of rhythm transformed this noise into a terrible melody, with the shore, vibrating under the shock of the waves, replying to the thunder of the open sea.

For a moment he wondered whether he should not end it all here: no one would see him, no rescue could be hoped for, in three minutes he would be dead. But then, with a contradiction usual at such moments, existence came to smile on him; his life in Paris seemed attractive, full of prospects: he saw his comfortable study and all the calm days he might yet pass there. And yet, the voices of the abyss called to him, the waves opened like a tomb, ready to close over him and wrap him in their watery folds. . . .

He was frightened. He went back. All that night he listened in terror to the whistling of the wind. He made an enormous fire and warmed himself at it until his legs were almost scorched.

His journey was over. Returning home, he found his windows white with hoarfrost; the coals were extinguished in the hearth, his clothes lay on the bed where he had left them, the ink had dried in the inkwell, the walls were cold and sweating.

"Why did I not stay out there?" he asked himself, and he thought bitterly of the joy of his setting forth.

Summer came, but brought him no joy. Now and then he stood on the Pont des Arts and watched the trees sway in the Tuileries and the rays of the setting sun, purpling the sky, pass in a shower of light beneath the Arch of the Etoile.

At length, last December, he died; but slowly, little by little, solely by the force of thought, without any organic malady, as one dies of sorrow—which may seem incredible to those who have greatly suffered, but must be tolerated in a novel, for the sake of our love of the marvellous.

He asked that his body be opened, for fear of being buried alive, but he absolutely refused to be embalmed.

FINE WORKS OF FICTION AND NON-FICTION AVAILABLE IN QUALITY PAPERBACK EDITIONS FROM CARROLL & GRAF

- [ ] Anderson, Nancy/WORK WITH PASSION
  $8.95 Cloth $15.95
- [ ] Appel, Allen/TIME AFTER TIME   Cloth $17.95
- [ ] Asch, Sholem/THE APOSTLE $10.95
- [ ] Asch, Sholem/EAST RIVER $8.95
- [ ] Asch, Sholem/MARY $10.95
- [ ] Asch, Sholem/THE NAZARENE
  $10.95 Cloth $21.95
- [ ] Asch, Sholem/THREE CITIES $10.50
- [ ] Asprey, Robert/THE PANTHER'S FEAST $9.95
- [ ] Athill, Diana/INSTEAD OF A LETTER
  $7.95 Cloth $15.95
- [ ] Babel, Isaac/YOU MUST KNOW EVERYTHING
  $8.95
- [ ] Bedford, Sybille/ALDOUS HUXLEY $14.95
- [ ] Bellaman, Henry/KINGS ROW $8.95
- [ ] Bernanos, Georges/DIARY OF A COUNTRY PRIEST $7.95
- [ ] Berton, Pierre/KLONDIKE FEVER $10.95
- [ ] Blanch, Lesley/PIERRE LOTI $10.95
- [ ] Blanch, Lesley/THE SABRES OF PARADISE$9.95
- [ ] Blanch, Lesley/THE WILDER SHORES OF LOVE
  $8.95
- [ ] Bowers, John/IN THE LAND OF NYX $7.95
- [ ] Buchan, John/PILGRIM'S WAY $10.95
- [ ] Carr, Virginia Spencer/THE LONELY HUNTER: A BIOGRAPHY OF CARSON McCULLERS $12.95
- [ ] Chekov, Anton/LATE BLOOMING FLOWERS
  $8.95
- [ ] Conot, Robert/JUSTICE AT NUREMBURG$10.95
- [ ] Conrad, Joseph/SEA STORIES $8.95
- [ ] Conrad, Joseph & Ford Madox Ford/THE INHERITORS
  $7.95

☐ Conrad, Joseph & Ford Madox Ford/ROMANCE
$8.95

☐ Cooper, Lady Diana/AUTOBIOGRAPHY $12.95
☐ de Montherlant, Henry/THE GIRLS $11.95
☐ de Poncins, Gontran/KABLOONA $9.95
☐ Edwards, Anne/SONYA: THE LIFE OF COUNTESS
TOLSTOY $8.95
☐ Elkington, John/THE GENE FACTORYCloth $16.95
☐ Farson, Negley/THE WAY OF A TRANSGRESSOR
$9.95

☐ Feutchwanger, Lion/JEW SUSS $8.95 Cloth $18.95
☐ Feutchwanger, Lion/THE OPPERMANS $8.95
☐ Feutchwanger, Lion/SUCCESS $10.95
☐ Fisher, R.L./THE PRINCE OF WHALES
Cloth $12.95

☐ Ford Madox Ford & Joseph Conrad/THE
INHERITORS $7.95
☐ Ford Madox Ford & Joseph Conrad/ROMANCE
$8.95

☐ Fuchs, Daniel/SUMMER IN WILLIAMSBURG
$8.95

☐ Gold, Michael/JEWS WITHOUT MONEY $7.95
☐ Goldin, Stephen & Sky, Kathleen/THE BUSINESS
OF BEING A WRITER $8.95
☐ Green, Julian/DIARIES 1928–1957 $9.95
☐ Greene, Graham & Hugh/THE SPY'S BEDSIDE
BOOK $7.95
☐ Hamsun, Knut/MYSTERIES $8.95
☐ Hawkes, John/VIRGINIE: HER TWO LIVES $7.95
☐ Haycraft, Howard (ed.)/THE ART OF THE
MYSTERY STORY $9.95
☐ Haycraft, Howard (ed.)/MURDER FOR PLEASURE
$10.95

☐ Ibañez, Vincente Blasco/THE FOUR HORSEMEN
OF THE APOCALYPSE $8.95
☐ Jackson, Charles/THE LOST WEEKEND $7.95
☐ James, Henry/GREAT SHORT NOVELS $11.95
☐ Lansing, Alfred/ENDURANCE: SHACKLETON'S
INCREDIBLE VOYAGE $8.95
☐ Leech, Margaret/REVEILLE IN WASHINGTON
$11.95

☐ Linder, Mark/THERE CAME A PROUD BEGGAR
Cloth $18.95

- [ ] Lowry, Malcolm/ULTRAMARINE $7.95
- [ ] Macaulay, Rose/CREWE TRAIN $8.95
- [ ] Macaulay, Rose/DANGEROUS AGES $8.95
- [ ] Macmillan, Harold/THE BLAST OF WAR $12.95
- [ ] Martin, Jay/NATHANAEL WEST: THE ART OF HIS LIFE $8.95
- [ ] Maurois, Andre/OLYMPIO: THE LIFE OF VICTOR HUGO $12.9
- [ ] Maurois, Andre/PROMETHEUS: THE LIFE OF BALZAC $11.95
- [ ] Maurois, Andre/PROUST: PORTRAIT OF A GENIUS $10.95
- [ ] McCarthy, Barry & Emily/SEXUAL AWARENESS $9.95
- [ ] McElroy, Joseph/LOOKOUT CARTRIDGE $9.95
- [ ] McElroy, Joseph/A SMUGGLER'S BIBLE $9.50
- [ ] Moore, George/THE LAKE $8.95
- [ ] Mizener, Arthur/THE SADDEST STORY: A BIOGRAPHY OF FORD MADOX FORD $12.95
- [ ] Montyn, Jan & Kooiman, Dirk Ayelt/A LAMB TO SLAUGHTER $8.95
- [ ] Mullins, Edwin/THE PAINTED WITCH Cloth $25.00
- [ ] Munro, H.H./THE NOVELS AND PLAYS OF SAKI $8.95
- [ ] Munthe, Axel/THE STORY OF SAN MICHELE $8.95
- [ ] O'Casey, Sean/AUTOBIOGRAPHIES I $10.95 Cloth $21.95
- [ ] O'Casey, Sean/AUTOBIOGRAPHIES II $10.95 Cloth $21.95
- [ ] O'Faolain, Julia/THE OBEDIENT WIFE Cloth $17.95
- [ ] Olinto, Antonio/THE WATER HOUSE Cloth $18.95
- [ ] Ormrod, Richard/UNA TROUBRIDGE: THE FRIEND OF RADCLYFFE HALL Cloth $18.95
- [ ] Plievier, Theodore/STALINGRAD $8.95
- [ ] Poncins, Gontran de/KABLOONA $9.95
- [ ] Proffitt, Nicholas/GARDENS OF STONE Cloth $14.95
- [ ] Proust, Marcel/ON ART AND LITERATURE $8.95

- Rechy, John/BODIES AND SOULS
  $8.95 Cloth $17.95
- Richelson, Hildy & Stan/INCOME WITHOUT TAXES   Cloth $16.95
- Rowse, A.L./HOMOSEXUALS IN HISTORY $9.95
- Roy, Jules/THE BATTLE OF DIENBIENPHU $8.95
- Russel, Robert A./WINNING THE FUTURE Cloth $16.95
- Russell, Franklin/THE HUNTING ANIMAL
  $7.95
- Salisbury, Harrison/A JOURNEY OF OUR TIMES
  $10.95
- Scott, Evelyn/THE WAVE $9.95
- Service, William/OWL $8.95
- Sigal, Clancy/GOING AWAY $9.95
- Silverstein, Fanny/MY MOTHER'S COOKBOOK
  Cloth $16.95
- Singer, I.J./THE BROTHERS ASHKINAZI $9.95
- Sloan, Allan/THREE PLUS ONE EQUALS BILLIONS $8.95
- Stein, Leon/THE TRIANGLE FIRE $7.95
- Taylor, Peter/IN THE MIRO DISTRICT $7.95
- Tolstoy, Leo/TALES OF COURAGE AND CONFLICT
  $11.95
- Wassermann, Jacob/CASPAR HAUSER $9.95
- Wassermann, Jacob/THE MAURIZIUS CASE $9.95
- Werfel, Franz/THE FORTY DAYS OF MUSA DAGH
  $9.95
- Werth, Alexander/RUSSIA AT WAR 1941–1945
  $15.95
- Wilmot, Chester/STRUGGLE FOR EUROPE $12.95
- Zuckmayer, Carl/A PART OF MYSELF $9.95

Available from fine bookstores everywhere

To order direct from the publishers please send check or money order including the price of the book plus $1.75 per title for postage and handling. N.Y. State Residents please add 8¼% sales tax.

Caroll & Graf Publishers, Inc.
260 Fifth Avenue, N.Y., N.Y. 10001